HER ALIEN MERCENARIES

SUSAN HAYES

SUSAN HAYES

Her Alien Mercenaries (Book 8 of the Drift: Haven Colony)

First Print: July 2024

Editor: Amanda Brown

Published by: Black Scroll Publications Ltd.

ABOUT THE BOOK

She thought that moving to a new world would be the challenge of a lifetime. Then the universe upped the ante.

Jenna never expected to escape from Earth. Now she's a colonist in a beautiful and inviting new world, surrounded by beings she wants to trust... if only she could.

Not everyone in Haven wants it to succeed, and Jenna is now a pawn in a dangerous game of secrets and subterfuge.

To protect her new home, she'll have to risk everything, including her chance at love.

They thought they could leave their bloodstained past behind them. They were wrong.

Zanyr and Torren may have kept their names, but they left the rest of their former lives behind. Most of their species despise mercenaries, which means they must hide their past to protect their future with the colony.

Their lives bound by blood-oaths and battle, these former soldiers of fortune want nothing more than to live in peace with their mate... once they find her, that is.

These three will have the chance to get everything they've ever wanted... but to keep it, they may have to go to war.

PROLOGUE

Beyond the edge of civilized space is a newly colonized planet. It's a haven for the homeless, the hopeful, and those dreaming of freedom.

The beings who live here might be different species from vastly different worlds, but they all have one thing in common. Whoever they are, and wherever they came from, Haven is now their home.

The land is uncharted. The dangers are unknown. It's a world full of possibilities—for those willing to risk everything.

Welcome to Haven Colony.

1

JENNA WOULD NEVER tire of being able to walk outside. No matter what the weather, she went out every day, even if only for a few minutes. The freedom to move under an open sky and breathe air that had never been recycled was a gift she would never take for granted.

Mornings were her favorite time to go out. Sometimes she'd wake up early enough to watch the sun rise. Seeing the sky lighten as color returned to the world reminded her of how she felt the first time she'd stepped foot on this planet. Until that moment, her existence had been all shades of gray. Now she knew there was more to life than her old self ever imagined. She reveled in every new experience, even the ones that scared her. Adjusting to a life under an open sky hadn't been easy. Not to mention that the dangerous wildlife and plants on this world gave her occasional nightmares.

Despite it all, Haven was everything she'd never dared to hope for, and so much more. Here, she could live instead of simply surviving. If she ever had to go back...

No. She tried to stop that line of thought before it could get any traction. If it happened, she'd find a way to cope. She always did. She might not have thrived in every situation the universe tossed at her, but she'd survived.

The little voice in the back of her head refused to be silenced. *But what if survival isn't enough? What if I want more than that?*

The thought tore through her like a comet plowing through an asteroid field—bright, beautiful, and leaving nothing but chaos in its wake. Her stride faltered, and the beautiful morning lost some of its color. But only for a moment.

She spoke her next words aloud, though softly enough that no one else could hear. "This is my home now. I'm never going back. I'm a full-fledged member of the colony."

The reminder helped. She and the other women selected to join Haven colony had completed the introductory training and assessment stage a week ago. Only a handful had washed out of the program along the way, with a single person opting to return to Earth. The others who hadn't made it were on their way to Defiance Station, out in the Drift. The station was still under construction, but Siva and the others had been offered jobs as support staff for the logistical infrastructure already in place.

They couldn't wait to get off the planet and back to a self-contained station. From her perspective, they were trading paradise for purgatory. Siva had laughed when she said so and pointed out that to some of the new arrivals, Haven was hell. The higher gravity, open skies, and even the weather had been too much for them to adapt to.

She'd miss them all. Well, most of them. Her lips pursed in a momentary grimace as she thought about the one person she would *not* miss. Reni. Unlike the others, Reni wouldn't be going back to Earth or out to the Drift. She was in a cell somewhere, locked away from everyone, including the mysterious cabal who had recruited her to spy for them.

Everyone was shocked when the news broke that another spy had been sent to Haven. The rest of the group had spent days and nights talking about it, trying to understand why she'd done it and how she'd been caught.

Jenna had speculated right along with them, her fury at the betrayal as real as everyone else's. The difference was she'd already figured out what Reni was up to. They'd been given the same offer by the same people back on Earth. But while Reni had chosen to accept it, Jenna had made a different choice. She'd risked her seat on the ship to Haven by reporting the offer a few hours after she'd received it.

Instead of losing her chance to escape, the Vardarians gave her an opportunity to protect her new home. She had to pretend to spy for this other group and report everything back to the Vardarians. She'd agreed, which made her the most unlikely double agent in existence.

The trouble with thinking too much was that you missed what was going on around you. While she'd been lost in thought, she'd managed to cover most of the distance to her destination. Winged forms soared overhead as the older children made their way to the education center. Laughter filled the air as they swooped and dove with reckless disregard for gravity or personal space.

The sidewalks were almost as busy as the air above as children too young to fly walked and chattered to each other, some of them looking up with obvious envy. None of them were human children, but the similarities struck her more so than the differences. Their laughter was high and light as they looked around with bright, curious expressions. A few looked dejected, their footsteps plodding and slow as they trudged along, some being coaxed by their parents or older siblings.

It was all so familiar, only this time she wasn't bringing her charges to school for the day. This time, she'd be joining them as one of their teachers.

Her being a teacher was almost as unbelievable as being a spy, yet here she was.

Several of the children, or younglings as the Vardarians called them, eyed her curiously as they entered the center's grounds. With less than fifty ordinary humans on the entire planet, she wasn't surprised by their interest. Oh, plenty of cyborgs were around. Several hundred, in fact. And every single one of them was physically perfect—not just in function but in appearance.

She often wondered if that had been deliberate or if the corporations that created the cybernetic soldiers had never intended for their creations to be as beautiful as they were deadly.

A silver-scaled Vardarian with blonde hair streaked with silver and a bright smile popped out of a doorway and hurried over to meet her. "You're right on time. Trying to make a good impression on your first day?" Director Saska Firt spoke in one of the more common dialects of Vardarian, but Jenna understood every word.

She shook her head and replied in the same language. "I think it would take more than that to impress you, Saska. I'm a morning person. Starting the day is easy for me. It's the long, sleepy stretch at the end of the evening that is always a challenge." She turned to smile at her new administrator. "Any last-minute advice for the newbie?"

Saska's pale green eyes gleamed with amusement as she lowered her voice to a playful whisper. "Don't be fooled by their adorable faces. All younglings are the same, no matter what species. If they sense weakness, they will exploit it. Stay strong."

Jenna nodded. "I'll do my best."

Saska patted her on the shoulder. "I know you will. You might be new to teaching, but you have years of experience under your wings. Oops." She winced. "Sorry. Wrong idiom. What do your people say? Under your feet?"

"Belt. We say under our belt." Jenna wrinkled her nose as she considered the expression. "I don't know why. To my mind, wings sounds much better."

The Vardarian female chuckled. "I would agree, but that would make me seem biased. Since you are the language expert, I will simply defer to your opinion."

Jenna still wasn't used to hearing herself described that way. On Earth, most people tried to minimize her abilities. They referenced her "knack for languages," or summarized her years of study as an interesting talent. On Earth everyone spoke Galactic Common no matter what hive city they lived in, which limited her usefulness, or so she was told.

She knew they were lying to her. Life in a hive city was predicated on power. The more you had, the more you lied and manipulated to keep it while gaining more. She'd never had any power at all, but she'd spent her entire adult life working for people who did. It left her with a collection of hard-earned lessons and a deep dislike for liars of any kind.

Including herself. Because that's what she was—a liar. Oh sure, it was for the best of reasons. She was doing her part to protect the colony and everyone in it, but that didn't change the facts.

Liar. Liar. Pants on fire. The children's ditty ran through her mind. Another strange saying from humanity's distant past. She didn't even know where she'd picked it up. Probably from one of the children she'd looked after. It wasn't likely she'd learned it during her own childhood. She tried not to dwell on those memories too much. Life in a corporate-sponsored care center provided her with food, shelter, and an education, but little else worth remembering.

Jenna realized her mind had wandered and refocused her attention on what Saska was saying. "... know you've toured the complex several times, but if you get turned around, you can always get directions from the central system."

"I'll remember that." Jenna doubted she'd get lost in the neatly laid out space. Vardarian architecture tended toward wide open spaces and flowing lines that felt both organic and logical.

"Good luck today. Your classroom is that way. I should get back to work..."

Whatever else Saska was about to say was drowned out by several delighted shrieks and cheers from above. Several late arrivals scattered to make way for an adult Vardarian male who approached the grounds from a dive so steep and fast she couldn't imagine how he'd stop in time to avoid getting hurt.

Jenna gasped, but Saska uttered a sound somewhere between a grunt and a sigh. "Typical. Torren will be late for his own funeral. Which will no doubt be brought about because he crashed into something while flying too fast."

"That's a *teacher?*" she asked. Her eyes were still locked on the male. At the last second, he extended his wings, catching the air and letting him turn his fall into an elegant swoop that ended with him soaring a short distance before setting down in an open space.

Saska huffed. "That is Torren Vex. He teaches science to the younger classes and chemistry to the senior students. Come on. I'll introduce you. That way you'll know who to blame when your classroom fills up with strange smelling smoke at some point. Believe me. It *will* happen."

Jenna watched with interest as he folded back his wings, making them vanish beneath the back of his loose-fitting tunic. The morning sunlight glinted off golden scales as he turned from the still cheering students to meet Saska's disapproving gaze.

Instead of looking apologetic, the male grinned and raised both wings in what she'd learned was the Vardarian version of a shrug.

Damn, he was hot. Exactly the kind of man she'd avoided back on Earth. It didn't matter that his long hair was tied back in a neat ponytail with only a few strands falling loose to frame a face that might have been sculpted by a master artisan. His clothes were relatively mundane by Vardarian standards, a simple black sleeveless top with only a bit of simple blue stitching along the rounded collar set over a pair of black pants.

It mattered not a whit that he looked neat, tidy, and professional. She knew what he was.

Trouble.

And stars above and below, he was staring at her like she was the last piece of bacon at a breakfast buffet.

"*Mahaya.*" He uttered the word with utter conviction and a hint of wonder, his voice so low it was more rumble than speech.

Jenna froze. What? No. This was her first day at her new job. She wasn't... this couldn't... *fraxx.*

Of course it could happen. It was happening. She'd been warned often enough. She just never imagined it would happen to *her.*

Saska looked from Torren to Jenna and back again, both brows raised almost to her hairline in shock. Then she swore softly and uttered a sigh. "Right then. I need to rearrange the schedules and find two beings to substitute for the two of you. I expect both of you to resume your duties next week once you get this..." She moved her hands through the air between them. "Sorted out. Good luck and congratulations."

Saska walked away, leaving Jenna standing with a tall, handsome as hell stranger... Who was apparently her *fraxxing* mate.

2

———

Hot water cascaded over his body, washing away the last traces of sleep and silencing the part of him that still wanted to go back to bed. Not that he needed the rest. Torren, like every other Vardarian in existence, was born with nanotech. The micro-machines optimized his body in every way imaginable, including metabolism, immunity, and how much sleep he needed. Despite all that, he still liked to sleep in as long as possible.

With a groan, he stretched his arms over his head and extended his wings so they reached from wall to wall. Space was a luxury he'd gone without for decades. It was one of the many things he loved about their new life in Haven. For the first time since leaving his parents' estates so many years ago, he had the two things he'd missed: space and privacy.

Thoughts of what he had now led to memories of his former life. His mind drifted as he recalled cramped bunks, stale air, and the constant buzz and bump of energy that only happened when too many people were crammed into a too-small space.

Sounds and scents came back to him. The too loud laughter that came right before a battle. The crackle and snap of a fresh ammo pack slammed into place. Copper in the air as a friend bled out. The screams of a stranger begging for someone to stop the pain. The gut-punch wallop of an explosion going off at close range.

When he opened his eyes, he wasn't in the shower anymore. He was trapped in a nightmare. He tried to move, to run, to fight, but all he could do was stand in the middle of a murky landscape as a torrent of hot blood flowed over him.

He started to scream, and it flooded his mouth. He choked, spat, and finally sucked in a lungful of air.

"It's not real!" he reminded himself. "Snap out of it. You're good. It's all good."

He muttered reassurances, one hand pressed against the smooth tiles along the nearest wall as he fought to ground himself. He went through one of the exercises he'd read about, taking each breath with purpose and holding it for a few seconds before exhaling. Three breaths, and he was calm enough to start cataloging sensations: the coolness of the tile beneath his hand, the sound of water pattering against the tile.

A few more deep breaths, and he found his center. Much better.

His newly established calm shattered when Zanyr's voice sounded in his head. *"Move your scaly ass or you'll be late. Again. Director Firt will string you up by your wings if you're late on the first day of the semester."*

"Chip, turn off the shower and activate the drying sequence."

The system chimed in acknowledgment. A moment later, warm air buffeted him from all sides.

Torren sped the process along by toweling himself off as he replied to his friend and blood-brother. *"I'll be down shortly. I'm moving slowly this morning."*

The internal comm link buzzed as Zanyr laughed. *"You move slowly every qarfing morning. If you're not here quick, I'm eating your breakfast. I've already had mine."*

"You're done already because you bolt your food with all the manners and restraint of a starving gharshtu. You probably didn't even taste your meal."

The banter helped to calm him, the same way it had when they'd done it during countless missions.

Had his *anrik* guessed Torren was having an episode? Probably not, but he was grateful for the distraction, anyway.

"My meal was delicious, thank you. Yours looks good too. Better hurry..."

A quick check of the time told him he really did need to get going. He jogged back to his bedroom to grab the clothes he'd laid out last night.

Dark pants, a well-tailored but simple tunic, and comfortable shoes. It wasn't much different from what he wore in his last career, only now he didn't need body armor or a half-dozen weapons to do his job.

With a grin, he scooped up his clothes and hurried back to the landing. Their bedrooms were on the second floor with a large open area that allowed anyone in a hurry to fly down to the main floor instead of taking the stairs.

The moment he took flight, Torren grinned. This was one of the advantages of living outside of the colony. They'd been allowed to build a home larger than those in town, with tall ceilings and wide-open spaces that flowed into each other, making it possible to fly from one side of the house to the other.

He touched down in the middle of the main living area and strode toward the kitchen, the smell of food making his stomach rumble.

"Took you long enough, I was..." Zanyr turned around, saw Torren, and scowled, baring his teeth enough to show his fangs.

To anyone who didn't know him, Zan probably looked terrifying. Torren knew him too well to worry, though. The only time he worried was when his *anrik* went quiet.

"*Qarf!* Why are you naked? It's in the rules, Vex. No nudity around the food."

Torren ignored his friend's bluster and went straight to the plate of food waiting on the counter. "Aren't you the one always claiming that rules were made to be broken?"

"Not this rule. We signed a contract and everything. House rules are to be respected." He gestured in Torren's general direction. "Now I'm nauseated and deeply regretting the sausages I had for breakfast. Put on some *fraxxing* clothes already."

"For a male who once went into a firefight naked, you're surprisingly uptight about nudity."

"That was for a bet. Plus, I was the only one naked. I'm gorgeous." He gestured to himself. "Tell me I'm wrong."

"You're delusional." Torren set his plate on the table and then took a moment to get dressed before eating. In truth, he knew his blood-brother was right. Neither of them had trouble attracting female attention, but Zanyr was the one they noticed first.

That hadn't changed since they'd come to Haven. Not that either of them had accepted any offers for company. They wanted something more than a temporary arrangement. They wanted a mate. Their mate. The one female in the galaxy they were destined for.

"What?" Zanyr asked. "No comeback? You're admitting I'm better looking?"

"I wouldn't go that far. You're not bad-looking. For a copper-back." He dropped the insult so casually it took a second for Zanyr to register he'd been disparaged.

"Asshole," he snapped, but he smiled as he said it. "I'll have you know that one of the new human females likes my coloring. She says it makes me distinctive."

The reddish cast to Zanyr's skin was the result of the hours he spent in the sun. Back in the empire, it would mark him as a laborer, beneath the notice of the upper classes. Attitudes like that were a large part of the reason Torren had left home as soon as he was of age. He'd been more than happy to put as many light years between him, his controlling family members, and his home system as possible.

"There's no accounting for human tastes. But out of curiosity, which one was it?"

"Nathalie, or something like that. She and a few of the others were at the market, trying to figure out what a *yakan* was and how to cook it. The vendor's translator was glitching, so I stepped in to help before they tried to boil the damned things and they exploded."

Torren snorted. "Bet they didn't cover that in their introductory courses."

"They should."

They both lapsed into silence while Torren tucked into his meal. When he was finished, he pushed the plate away and nodded to his friend. "Thanks for making breakfast. I was on schedule this morning until..." He trailed off and hoped Zanyr would understand.

He did.

"I figured. You were yelling in your sleep last night, too. Bad nights usually mean rough mornings for you."

"Sorry if I woke you." He'd been shouting? Torren couldn't decide if it was a good thing or a bad sign that he didn't remember anything about it.

"You didn't. I was already awake."

Which meant Zanyr had a rough night, too. They shared a look that spoke more than words ever could, and then Torren got to his feet. "You made breakfast. I'll take care of dinner."

"Deal. And tonight, we're going flying. Been too long since we've raced the winds."

"Good idea. Been a few weeks since we both had a bad night. Think there will ever come a time we don't think about the past anymore?"

"Sure." Zanyr didn't sound convinced. "It will probably happen right after we find our *mahaya*. Maybe we'll even manage to win our money back from Yardan the same day. He can't win *every* time we play cards."

"Sure he can. He cheats. Spymasters are not to be trusted."

"But he's on our side."

Zanyr snorted. "Not when it comes to cards."

It took him half a minute to clear his dishes and wash his hands. "See you tonight." He extended his arm, his hand turned so that the scar on the back of his wrist was visible.

They crossed wrists, pressing their scars, the mark of their blood-bond, together.

"Fair winds and clear skies," Zanyr said.

"Same to you, brother. We'll get through it." How many times had they said that to each other? Probably a thousand or more.

"We always do."

With that, Torren hurried off. If the winds were right, he'd arrive on time and Saska would have nothing to complain about... but when was his luck that good?

For once, the winds were perfect. He arrived almost two minutes faster than usual. That was more than enough time for him to get to his classroom, and thanks to good planning and some time spent at the school last night, he had nothing left to do but show up and teach.

Students of every age lingered outside, all of them

loath to enter the building and begin the first day of school. Some of them cheered as he touched down, while others stared in surprise. Torren was well aware of his reputation among the younglings. According to Director Firt, they viewed him with a mixture of respect and admiration combined with a hint of fear. As far as he was concerned, that was the ideal balance.

He spotted the director in the courtyard and turned toward her, raising his wings in a shrug. He wasn't late, and that was all that mattered.

The wind shifted at that moment, ruffling his hair and making it necessary to tug at the bottom of his tunic so it fell properly. The director was a stickler for two things—punctuality and professionalism. He could get away with lateness from time to time, but only if he looked and acted as she deemed proper.

The female had missed her calling. She should be running a military camp, not a school for younglings. Then again, given her commanding air and acid tongue, perhaps she had been in the military at some point. That would explain a lot.

His musings slammed to an ungainly halt as he caught a new scent on the wind. Hunger tore through him, as if he hadn't eaten in days. What the *fraxx*?

That scent. He didn't recognize it, but it called to him, demanding his attention. Desire sank sharp talons into his insides. Instantly, his cock hardened, the hunger deepening into something more. Something...

It wasn't until his scales tightened and he could hear the blood pounding in his ears that he understood what was happening. *She* was here. Somewhere.

He scanned the courtyard, seeking the source of the scent. Was this actually happening? It must be, but part of his mind still argued he had to be mistaken. Here? Now? He'd worked with these people for a year now. None of them were...

He finally saw her. The human held so still he hadn't noticed her standing beside the director, almost vanishing into Saska's shadow.

Quiet. Wary. Watching him intently. Did she already sense what was happening? Torren doubted it. Humans had never experienced anything like the *sharhal*, the mating fever, until coming into contact with his race. They would have to remember. This would not be a simple claiming.

He laughed to himself. What was he saying? He'd never heard of a simple, straightforward claiming. Mating and war were much the same in that regard. Neither process ever went according to plan.

He'd covered half the distance between them before he even realized he had moved. The closer he got, the stronger her scent, and the more certain he was.

"Mahaya." The word came unbidden, a statement of fact. She was his mate. Their mate. The one they'd been waiting on for so long they'd started to give up hope.

The female stiffened, her eyes—brown, he noted, warm and expressive—widening as he approached. More details came to him. Her face was lovely with delicate features, and her hair was dark, long enough that she'd braided and bound into a knot at the back of her neck. The way she held herself made her seem shorter than she actually was, though he still towered over her. She was slender, too. With long limbs and subtle curves hidden beneath her loose-fitting outfit.

He barely noticed when the director addressed them, only catching the second half of whatever she said.

"I expect both of you to resume your duties next week once you get this..." She moved her hands through the air between them. "Sorted out. Good luck and congratulations."

"Thank you," he called out as Saska moved purposely through the crowd of curious younglings.

One of them took a step in his direction, and alarms sounded in the back of his mind. Curiosity would lead to questions, and questions would mean delays. That was unacceptable.

He held out his hand to her, overriding the urge to scoop her into his arms and take off before anyone could stop him. "We need to leave."

She reached for his hand but stopped before they made contact. "Why?"

He did his best to sound calm and rational, which he thought was damn impressive, given he was anything but. "If we don't depart now, the younglings will figure out what's happened."

"Oh." She nodded, the skin on her cheeks darkening slightly. "You're trying to protect their innocence. Of course. I should have thought of that."

She placed her small hand in his, the softness of her skin making it almost impossible for him to think.

"Uh. What?" His brain managed to catch up. "What part? The *sharhal?*" He chuckled. "They know all about the mating fever. We are much more open about such things than humans, I think. I want to avoid their questions."

She glanced around, her eyes widening as she noticed they were the center of attention.

"Oh! Oh no. Uh, I mean yes. Yes, we should go. *Now*." To his amusement, she tried to pull him along with her as she made for the gate leading outside.

He resisted her, not completely, but enough to slow her down. "Easy. If you bolt, they'll be on us like a ghost cat on a squeaker."

She took a quick breath and nodded once. "Right. Don't show weakness. That's what Director Firt told me."

The younglings closed in, and Torren knew the possibilities for escape were dwindling. "Apologies for rushing this, but we're out of options. Hang on, blossom. I'll get us somewhere we can talk."

He tugged her closer and then crouched, gathering her into his arms. Instead of acting shocked or even surprised, the female laughed and flung her arms around his neck. "Go, quickly. Before I come to my senses."

Everywhere their bodies touched felt as if it had been seared by flames. He wanted to relish this moment, but that wasn't a good idea. With his mate held tightly in his arms, he spread his wings and launched into the air, every downbeat of his wings lifting them higher.

Noises of disappointment followed them, but in seconds they were over the walls and away.

Without a communication link, the only way to speak to his mate was by shouting. Since that would allow others on the ground to hear, he opted to say nothing for now. At least, not to her.

However, he needed to speak to someone else.

"Zan. I found her." He sent the subvocalized message via their private channel. Even as he spoke, he knew no words could convey the importance of this moment. *Her.* She was here. They'd found her.

Strike that. He'd found her. And he'd never let Zanyr forget it.

"Say again? Found who?"

Torren grinned to himself and dragged out his next words. *"I found our mahaya."*

He counted off the seconds while Zanyr processed what he'd said. It took the male nearly five seconds to speak again. *"You're sure?"*

"I've never been more certain of anything in my life. Drop what you're doing and meet us."

"Where are you?"

He didn't feel like explaining that he'd fled from a bunch of curious students. Instead, he glanced down and tried to figure out a good place to land—somewhere quiet but maybe not too private. The female probably wouldn't be comfortable if she found herself alone with two unknown males claiming to be her mates.

"Meet us outside the Bar None. Oh, and let Saral know we'll need a table in the back. If she makes a fuss, tell her why."

Zanyr laughed. *"She'll throw out some poor unsuspecting fool and clear the table herself if I do that. I know what she's like when it comes to matings. Speaking of, are you going to tell me our mahaya's name?"*

"I would if I knew it. We haven't had time for introductions yet. Get your ass in the air already."

"I'm airborne. What can you tell me about her? Something. Anything."

Torren looked down at the delicate female curled against his chest and felt a thrum of possessive desire that made it hard to think.

"She's beautiful, Zan. She's also..." He trailed off as his attention wavered and he gave in to the temptation to nuzzle the crown of her hair.

"Also what? If you don't finish that sentence, I will break off one of your wings and beat you with it when next we meet."

Torren chuckled to himself, amused by his *anrik's* frustration. *"She's human."*

3

———

SHE WAS out of her mind. That had to be it. There was
no other possible explanation for what she was doing.
Why else would she be flying over the colony in the arms
of an impossibly attractive stranger?

Maybe it was a dream? Jenna considered the
possibility, but her dreams were never this vivid. From
the wind rushing by her ears to the feel of his scales
beneath her hands, everything screamed to her that this
was real. And if that was the case, this was happening.
She'd found her mate. No, she corrected herself. Mates.
Plural.

That thought triggered a rush of increasingly graphic
images. Her with two males. Naked. Friction. Hands
stroking, mouths... *whoa*. It took more time and effort
than she expected to tear her attention away from the
rich fantasies filling her head. Despite the cool wind, she
felt overheated, every part of her sizzling with the need to
touch and be touched in turn.

She buried her face against his chest, using his body

to stifle the low moan that tore from her throat as her clit began to throb in time to her pounding heart.

It took three deep breaths before she felt like she was in control again and three more before her higher brain functions kicked in and she could think with relative clarity. It wasn't ideal, but it was an improvement. Jenna kept a handle on her anxiety by ensuring she was always aware and in control of herself. Staying unobtrusive and unremarkable was the only real protection she'd had back on Earth. As one of the "staff," she'd been expected to enhance her employers' lives by managing to do her job and remain invisible as much as possible.

But that was on Earth. She wasn't there anymore, and the old rules didn't apply. Shadow, Skye, and the other females had prepared all the new colonists for this possibility. She knew what to expect. They all did. It was just that she'd never imagined it would happen to *her*.

Jenna went through what she knew about the *sharhal*. The mating fever was triggered by pheromones. It was unstoppable and irreversible, binding strangers together in a lifelong bond. It involved none of the courtship and complications of choice that came with human bonding. In theory, it sounded amazing. Who wouldn't want a relationship that guaranteed there'd be no interest in any other being? No cheating. No doubts.

Now that she was experiencing it in reality, though, she felt more than a little fear. What if her mates didn't like her? Or worse, what if they were somehow involved with the beings who had tried to recruit her as a spy?

Damn it to the stars. She needed to talk to Maggie and find out who they were and if she was safe with them. Why hadn't that occurred to her before she'd agreed to fly off with—what was his name again?—Torren. Yes. That was it. She had no idea who his *anrik* was, but he had to have one. Nearly every Vardarian male had a blood-brother.

What would he be like? *Veth*, what were either of them like? Saska didn't seem concerned about leaving her alone with Torren, so that had to mean he was a decent male. And he was a teacher. Species and cultural differences aside, no one wanted unpleasant or cruel beings around their offspring.

Once they could talk, she'd get to know him better. When would that be? And, for that matter, where were they going?

Raising her head, she shouted, "Where are you taking me?" But the wind tore her words away the moment they left her lips.

Determined, she tried again, this time tangling her fingers in the soft fabric of his vest and levering herself up close to his ear. Only, she didn't repeat her question. Instead, she traced the curve of his ear with her lips. Despite the wind, she caught a tantalizing whiff of his scent, something that reminded her of the first time she'd walked through the local woods. Whatever it was, she liked it. A fresh surge of desire made her want to laugh and kiss him at the same time. Never in her life had she felt like this, and she wanted to keep feeling this way.

Torren turned his head toward her and nuzzled her cheek. Instantly her stomach was full of butterflies, only these must have been mutants because they felt like small spacecraft buzzing around inside her.

They stayed like that for what might have been a few seconds or a few minutes. She had no way to tell. Being this close to him consumed all her attention.

It wasn't until he tapped her on the shoulder that she snapped out of whatever strange thrall she'd fallen into. Once he had her attention, he pointed down.

The colony stretched out beneath them, cream and white buildings laid out in perfectly ordered squares. Each one had at a park or open area in the center, every one of them different from the others. Tile mosaics decorated some of the buildings and made repeated patterns along the walkways while murals adorned the walls near street level, adding splashes of vibrant color and giving each neighborhood its own personality.

Beyond the colony was an impossibly wide expanse of green. In some places the land was cultivated for crops while in others it looked completely untouched. Fields gave way to forests that stretched all the way to the distant mountains in one direction while in the other...

She caught a glint of sunlight reflected off of water. So much water. Was that the *ocean*? She'd seen maps, of course, and knew the colony was less than fifty kilometers from the sea, but knowing wasn't the same as actually seeing it for herself.

She twisted and turned, but try as she might, she couldn't see more than the distant gleam of sun on water, so she turned her attention back to the immediate area. She spotted the river that bisected the two halves of the colony along with the bridge that connected the two sides. It was wide enough to allow for buildings, mostly market stalls and other semipermanent structures, to line both sides and still have room for pedestrians and traffic down the middle.

Torren pointed again, and she recognized their destination immediately. They were going to the Bar None, a human-owned tavern. That made her feel better. She wasn't ready to be alone with her new mates yet. Though part of her was already wondering what that would be like... because she knew it would happen. *Soon.*

One thing she'd discovered during their flight was that Haven had more living space than she'd assumed. Almost every rooftop they'd flown over had at least a few pieces of furniture and other comforts. Many of them had gardens as well, adding even more color and perhaps even landmarks for those flying overhead.

Why hadn't she considered that before? A species capable of flight would see perspectives no human would consider. The thought reminded her how far away from Earth she was, and how lucky she was to be here.

She'd always wanted this, a life that allowed for different perspectives and the opportunity to experience them for herself.

He set down on the roof of the Bar None, the landing surprisingly gentle. Planters edged three sides of the area, all of them full of carefully tended plants, some of which she actually recognized. Basil. Oregano. Mint. It was a kitchen garden, though on a scale she'd never seen back on Earth.

Instead of bending over to set her back on her feet, Torren released her legs first and then let her slide down the front of his body. She gasped at the delicious friction of the movement.

When she looked up at Torren, he grinned down at her, utterly unrepentant.

"I was right. You *are* trouble," she said in Galactic Common.

His smile only widened. "You are an astute judge of character, my *mahaya*," he replied in the same language. Unlike most of the others on the planet, Jenna didn't need a translator implant, which meant she heard every word as it was spoken with no electronic interference. Torren's voice was deep, confident, and lilted in a way she'd never heard during her studies of the main Vardarian languages.

"Ah, there he is. Late as always." Torren tipped his head and glanced up, drawing her attention to a rapidly approaching golden shape in the sky.

"He's your *anrik*?" she asked, suddenly nervous.

"He is. Though I'm certain he'd prefer it if you called him your *mahoyen*." The big male glanced down at her and took her hand in his. "As would I."

Jenna nodded and squeezed his hand. "*My mahoyen*."

Torren made a low rumbling sound of satisfaction and tightened his hold on her hand. "Yes, we are. And now, I want to know your name."

The request surprised her. Hadn't anyone mentioned her name yet? A quick replay of the day's events revealed that she'd never introduced herself. Neither had Torren, but she'd learned his name from Saska before the *sharhal* had slammed into her plans like a runaway starship.

"I'm sorry. I should have introduced myself." She

started to hold out her hand in greeting and then realized he was already holding it. "I'm Jenna."

"No apologies. I didn't introduce myself either." Torren glanced skyward and then raised her hand to his lips and kissed her fingers gently. "I am Torren Vex. And the golden blur headed our way is Zanyr Sallesh."

She tensed and glanced up at the sky again. "Zanyr? He's on the leadership council. Isn't he?"

Stars above and below. Was she mated to one of the colony's leaders? She was accustomed to dealing with beings of high rank and authority, but only a member of the staff. Would he be like them? Had she come all this way only to wind up in the same situation?

Torren snorted. "Yes, he was foolish enough to agree to serve as part of the council. You know the council has equal representation from all the species on Liberty with beings from diverse backgrounds. Someone managed to convince him to represent the agriculturists." Torren smirked. "So now he has to attend meetings and listen to long presentations while I enjoy quiet evenings at home."

Agriculturist? Jenna wanted to ask for more details, but Zanyr was only a few seconds away. Questions would have to wait.

Unlike Torren's earlier arrival, Zanyr's descent was controlled in both velocity and accuracy. He touched down lightly, the wind from his wings fanning her face and making the skirt of her dress flutter around her calves.

She hadn't had much time to envision what Zanyr might look like, but what she'd conjured in her mind had little in common with the reality. Instead of a well-dressed, refined male of power and influence, her mate was all rough edges and raw force of personality.

He wasn't quite as tall as Torren, but his build was broader across the chest and shoulders. His *bare* chest. She noted. Golden scales with a reddish cast gleamed brightly as he turned to face her. She knew what that meant. Either he was aroused, or he sensed danger. Her money was on the former.

She looked her fill, taking in the hard planes of his body and the way his stomach showed ridges of hard muscle. She could have wrapped both hands around one of his biceps and not made her fingers meet.

At first she thought his hair was blond but then quickly realized it was darker, with blond highlights that could only come from long hours spent outside. He had it cut short at the sides but with enough length on top for it to sweep across his forehead.

When her eyes met his, her heart did a little stutter step in her chest. His gaze was as bright as a laser, and the amber color of his eyes contrasted with the rim of black around irises and slightly oval pupils.

Torren broke the silence before it went on too long. "You took your time. Was there a headwind or are you getting old?" he asked, his tone as dry as moon dust.

"You barely beat me here," Zanyr argued. "And in case you forgot, I'm younger than you. Better looking, too." He folded back his wings and smoothed back his hair with one hand.

"Yes, but I was carrying the most precious of cargo. Zanyr, this is Jenna. Our *mahaya*."

She reached out her hand, but Zanyr ignored it.

Instead, he crossed the space between them and then dropped to one knee, his gaze locked on her face. "*Mahaya.* With the breath of my lungs, I welcome you into our lives."

She should have said something eloquent, or at least intelligent, but all Jenna managed was an incoherent squeak. Anxiety locked up her lungs and froze her brain. Part of her wanted to flee, to hide from all this attention. This was such an important moment, and she was screwing it up.

Stupid, she chided herself. *Why am I always so stupid and useless?*

She curled her fingers into fists and dug her nails into her palms. The pain pushed back the momentary panic, and she knew what to do.

"Hello, Zanyr," she greeted him in his language. "May the ancestors bless this meeting and grant all of us fair winds in our travels together."

Both males stared at her, frozen.

"You speak our language?" Torren asked a second before Zanyr asked the same question.

"I speak several dialects of Vardarian," she said, fighting to keep her voice calm and even. She would not, could not, screw this up any more than she already had.

"You speak it well," Zanyr added, his lips quirking into an approving smile as he rose to his feet. "Our *mahaya* is as smart as she is beautiful."

The unexpected compliment made her cheeks burn. He thought she was beautiful?

Torren shot the other male an amused look. "And

here I thought you'd forgotten how to be charming. Have you been practicing on your plants?"

Zanyr made a rude gesture with one hand but never took his eyes off her. His nostrils flared, his next inward breath loud enough for her to hear it clearly. "You smell like raindrops on drought-stripped soil. Gentle, soothing, and full of promise. You *are* our *mahaya*."

Torren made a noise somewhere between a snort and a growl. "You doubted me?"

Zanyr shot Torren a wicked grin that made her pulse quicken again. Damn it, they both had bad-boy vibes. She was doomed.

"Doubt you? Never. How could I when you keep telling me you're always right?"

Jenna giggled. She hadn't meant to, but her emotions were all over the place, and her nerves were shot.

Both males turned to her, fixing her with smoldering gazes that made what little of her brain still functioned start to melt away. "Sorry. The way you talk to each other is endearing."

"Endearing?" Zanyr looked horrified.

Torren scowled. "I don't believe anyone has ever described us that way before."

She bowed her head slightly, afraid that she'd offended them. "It's not bad. It's... well, cute." *Veth*. She was making this worse. "I mean, it's clear you are fond of each other. Like brothers. Teasing each other and pushing buttons."

Damn it, would they even understand what she meant? Colloquialisms rarely translated well. "Did that make sense to you?"

Zanyr nodded. "I take your meaning. He's my brother. Bound by blood and vow."

"I'm glad you see it for what it is. Our banter is just that. We don't mean anything by it." He paused before adding, "Most of the time."

She smiled at that, the next words coming out of her mouth before she thought them through. "You two are like the brothers I always wished I had."

Their good mood vanished immediately. "Oh no. He is my brother. *Not* yours, *ana-thi*. We are your mates," Zanyr growled. He took her by the hand and pulled her toward him.

Torren moved behind her, his hands on her hips as he pressed up against her, guiding her into Zanyr's embrace. "Allow us to demonstrate the difference."

Lust poured through her, as raw and real as anything she'd ever experienced. A small voice shouted at her to run and hide before the predators stalking her could pounce. For most of her life, that's what she'd done— hidden from threats and avoided the attentions of dangerous beings as much as possible.

Not this time. Something inside her whispered this time the dangerous predators belonged to *her*.

Fraxx it. She rose on her toes to kiss Zanyr's chin. She wasn't short, but he was big. Tall. Broad. Solid. She rested her hands on his bare chest as her lips brushed over his stubbled skin. "Not my brothers. Got it."

"I don't think you do because that was not nearly enough." Zanyr lowered his head, his mouth claiming hers in a kiss that seared her down to her soul.

"I doubt we'll ever get enough," Torren said, his

hands tightening on her waist as he rocked his hips against her backside.

Both males were aroused. She could feel the hard lengths of their cocks pressed up against her, front and back. Zanyr's kiss went on and on, his mouth hot and lips firm as he laid claim to her.

Torren nuzzled at her ear, his breath fanning her skin and sending ripples of goose bumps chasing down her spine.

Hands stroked her shoulders, her face, and her neck. She had no idea who was touching her where. Something whispered that she should be ashamed of that, but she wasn't. How could she be when it all felt so right?

Breathless and giddy with desire, her knees nearly gave way as Torren pulled her from Zanyr's embrace and turned her to face him. The look in his eyes stole her breath away. He wanted her. She could see it. Feel it. They both did.

Something new blossomed in her chest, a feeling she'd never known before. Belonging. They wanted her. Shy, ordinary, her. The one her first employers had called the Mouse. She'd hated the name, but over time she'd embraced it. That way of living kept her safe, unseen and, therefore, uninteresting.

That wasn't true anymore. Not with Zanyr and Torren. They *saw* her.

It was the most wonderful, terrifying feeling in all the worlds.

4

––––––

When Torren said he'd found their *mahaya*, Zanyr hadn't truly believed it was possible. Though he'd never spoken about it, Zanyr believed their ancestors were punishing them for the choices they'd made. Fighting for money was no life for a warrior with honor. No matter why they'd chosen that path, they'd never find their mate or lasting happiness until they chose a new direction.

Despite his uncertainty, he'd dropped what he was doing and rushed to their designated meeting place. Apart from a quick wash in an irrigation cistern, he'd not bothered with anything else. If she were truly their mate, she wouldn't care about appearances. And maybe a human female wouldn't judge them for the things they'd done in the past.

Maybe.

The moment he caught her scent, he'd known. All his doubts vanished, leaving him to bask in a moment of pure certainty. They'd found her. At long last, the ancestors had forgiven them and sent them a gift, carried on the fairest of winds.

He'd had his share of lovers over the years. They both had. Sometimes they'd shared while other times they'd enjoyed pleasurable company on their own, but neither of them had ever had more than a passing interest in the females they spent time with. Sex was a release, a distraction from the darkness that shrouded their lives. Jenna was so much more than that. She was their *mahaya*, the one female they would cherish and protect for the rest of their lives. And for Zanyr, she represented something more—redemption.

They kept her on the rooftop longer than he'd intended. The first kiss wasn't enough. Nor was the second. Or the third. Back and forth she'd moved between them, turned one way and then the other, until the need for her was a living flame. Torren had been right to bring her somewhere public, where they couldn't give in to the temptation to strip her naked and learn how to make her scream with pleasure.

Soon they'd do that. Soon, but not yet. That much had been drilled into them by those with human mates. They needed more time to adjust and accept the *sharhal* along with what it meant. Someone had mentioned gifting their mate with flowers. One of the cyborgs? Yes. Wreckage had done that.

He didn't know why plants were a good courtship gift, but he was an agriculturalist. He had plenty of plants he could offer. Whatever she wanted, whatever she needed, he'd find a way to get it for her.

"We should take her downstairs. If we stay any longer..." Torren messaged.

Zanyr agreed, but even then, it took several more minutes for them to stop.

By then, their *mahaya* was radiant, her eyes glowing with desire and her lips swollen from their kisses.

Once free, Jenna seemed to diminish, the light in her eyes dimming as she straightened out her clothes and tried to smooth back the strands of hair that had escaped the knot at the back of her head. "Give me a moment. I need to make myself presentable."

This time, she spoke in Galactic Common, her words muffled because she kept her head down. He didn't understand what had changed, but he didn't like it. Where had the passionate female who had kissed him gone, and why?

"You look beautiful." Torren took her hands to still them, his expression showing he was as concerned by the change as Zanyr.

"You are more than presentable, *ana-thi*. You are stunning and perfect. Why would you think otherwise?"

She raised her head and blinked at them in surprise. "I'm far from perfect. And what will everyone think if I show up looking like..." She gestured at herself. "This."

They will think that you were enjoying the attention of your *mahoyen*," Zanyr replied.

"While wishing they stood in our place. Well, the ones who do not have mates of their own." Torren smiled down at her. "And even some of them will be envious."

The wide-eyed look she gave them told Zanyr all he

needed to know. Jenna was uncertain. Was it them? The situation? Something else? He had no idea.

She tugged at her hands, trying to free herself from Torren's grip. "But I—"

He didn't let her finish. "No buts. We speak the truth. You are perfect, and to be blunt, I like that every male who sees you will know that we put that flush on your cheeks and covered you with our scent. He leaned down to gaze into her eyes. "You are ours."

Her pupils dilated and her teeth closed on her lower lip as she considered his words. Then she nodded. "Alright then. I don't think I can do any better than this, anyway."

This time, Torren released her hands when she pulled at them. She smoothed her hair with one hand, tucking the loose strands behind her ears. He was tempted to muss her up all over again, but now wasn't the time. He didn't understand the source of her doubts yet. He needed more information.

"Come." He held out his hand to her.

She took it without hesitation. "What happens now?"

He pulled her toward him, crouched, and swept her up into his arms. "Now, we go down to the tavern and spend some time getting to know each other."

"You're going to carry me? Oh no, no, no. I can walk."

"You can, yes. But I'd rather carry you." He grinned at her. "Indulge me?"

Her uncertainty broke like waves on the shore, replaced by a soft laugh and a smile that eclipsed the sun. "Indulging you sounds like a dangerous thing to do." Her small hand touched his cheek. "But I trust you." She glanced over at Torren. "And you as well."

Her words hit with the impact of a runaway rocket. His desire rekindled, amplified by new feelings that he didn't want to examine right now.

"You honor me," was all he said.

"You honor both of us," Torren said.

"If I can't trust my *mahoyen*, this mating is doomed before it even begins. I need to trust you." She looked down, avoiding his eyes as she spoke. "Isn't that how this works?"

Zanyr didn't know how to answer her. He wanted her trust, but he also wanted to earn it. If she knew who he'd been once, the things he'd done, would she trust him then? Looking down at his female, Zanyr made a decision. They couldn't tell her about their past. Not yet.

He carried her down the stairs while Torren filled the silence with inane chatter. They still spoke in their own language, confident she could understand them.

"Saral has a table waiting for us. They're not officially open yet, but she knows we're coming."

"They're not open yet? So it won't be busy? Just us?"

"I gather a few patrons come in early, but it won't be busy. Anya might not be much for mornings, but no one is going to turn away a paying customer."

"It's a bit early for her. She's not much for mornings, but I was told that Maggie is working already."

"Oh! I know Maggie. She taught a few classes on colony life and tricks to help us adapt." Jenna relaxed in his arms, apparently reassured now that someone she knew would be present. That it was another human female probably didn't hurt, either.

The stairs led to a small alleyway that ran alongside the tavern. The door to the kitchen was propped open, allowing a combination of savory scents to fill the air. Despite having already eaten, Zanyr's mouth watered. Unlike most taverns he'd come across in his life, the Bar None served excellent food that drew a crowd day after day.

Saral appeared in the doorway before they reached it. The Vardarian female greeted them with a spatula in her hand and a broad smile. "I was about to send one of my mates to the roof to see if you were ever coming down. Come in. Come in. Your table is ready."

Her gaze fell on Jenna, and her smile grew wider still. "Jenna! Congratulations. The winds have carried you into the lives of two of my favorite customers!"

"You claim everyone is your favorite customer," Torren pointed out as they filed into the kitchen.

"Because it's true. You all bring something special to this place. Even Thrash, but please don't tell him I said that. That male's ego is big enough already."

"Are you sure it's okay for us to be here? I mean, you're not even open yet," Jenna said as Zanyr navigated the bustling kitchen space, careful to keep a safe distance from the hot stove as well as the two males already hard at work.

"Of course! Anya may not love mornings, but we do."

Antas, the older of the two males, raised his head and winked. "I do like mornings. Especially the ones we aren't working. That way, we can keep our *mahaya* in bed all day."

Jenna blushed, but Saral laughed and blew a kiss to her mate. "Your *mahaya* likes that, too. In fact, I will tell Anya we need a few extra days off next week."

"More than one?" they asked at the same time.

"Of course. Like mates and orgasms, days off are better when they come in multiples." Saral chortled as she led them through the swinging door and into the main room.

A human female crouched behind the bar, both hands inside one of the bartending droids. "Ignore her, Jenna. Saral loves trying to embarrass humans. She thinks it's funny that we're so reserved about some things. And congratulations."

Zanyr looked down and noted that Jenna's cheeks had indeed darkened several shades.

"Thanks, Maggie. I guess this means I'm the first of the second group of colonists to experience the *sharhal*."

"Seems so. I haven't heard about anyone else falling prey to their pheromones yet. Which means your group will be bombarding you with questions the second they hear the news." Maggie shoved her red hair back from her face and straightened up. "You might want to turn off your comm before word gets out."

"*Veth*. That's a good idea. I'll do that." She turned and looked up at Zanyr. "As soon as someone puts me down."

"Good luck with that," Torren joked. "If he puts you down before we reach our table, I'm picking you right back up again."

Maggie snickered. "Welcome to the possessive males' possession club. We meet every second Tuesday afternoon here at the bar. No mated males allowed."

"Then we'll wait for her outside," Zanyr declared. No way was their *mahaya* going anywhere without them. She was theirs, and they would protect her at all costs.

Maggie shrugged. "You and every other newly mated male are welcome to lurk outside. Saral will even feed you if you ask her nicely, but you have to stay outside."

Torren scowled at Saral. "You won't let us inside?"

"Those are Anya's rules. I just enforce them." Saral chuckled and showed them to a table at the back of the large room. A few customers were already eating, and several Vardarians glanced up with curiosity. When each realized what was going on, they gave smiles and nods of acknowledgment of their good fortune.

The Bar None wasn't a flashy place. The furniture was standard, prefabricated stuff made to endure constant use without needing to be replaced. The ceilings were high enough to accommodate the taller-than-human height of most Vardarians, and the chairs were a mix of styles that allowed a variety of builds and species to sit down comfortably.

"Sit," Saral instructed. "I'll be back with your meals. Nothing too heavy. I don't expect you'll be hanging around long enough to eat much."

Torren pulled out a chair as Zanyr reluctantly set Jenna back on her feet.

"Wait. Saral. We didn't order anything yet."

The silver-scaled female chuckled as she walked away. "Trust me. I know what you want already."

"Well, okay then. I guess today is a two-breakfast day."

Zanyr claimed the seat to Jenna's left. "We often let her decide for us. She knows her customers well."

"But I've only met her once or twice." Jenna glanced over at the now-closing door. "You're sure?"

"Very," Torren stated. "You can trust Saral completely. In fact, if you have any questions about all of this that you don't want to ask us, she's the one you should talk to. That female is one of Haven's greatest treasures."

"Yes, she is. Every community needs someone like her." This tavern always made him think back to the better parts of his youth. It reminded him of his father's kitchen—comfortable, practical, and filled with the same rich scents of food.

He could almost hear his mother singing whatever new song they were learning at the local choir as she went about her chores. He let the fragments of memory flow through his mind, each one polished until they lost the rough edges of reality and shone with a glow only time and distance could create.

Jenna shook her head. "If she's all that, I certainly could have used someone like her back on Earth." The little human sighed. "I should mention that I'm an orphan. I was raised in a corporate-run institution. There's not a lot of kindness or wisdom to be found in places like that."

It felt as if a band of pure ice constricted his chest. From what he knew, Earth's hive cities were overcrowded, poverty-stricken places that were closer to breeding colonies for the corporations' workforces than anything else. What had she gone through growing up in such a place with no one to watch over her and keep her safe?

Without thinking, he reached out and took her hand. "I can't promise you wisdom. Torren and I have made too many mistakes in our lives to be considered wise, but I can promise you this. You will be safe with us, Jenna."

"Yes," Torren agreed. "You are ours, and we will protect you, support you, and do our best to make you happy."

Jenna smiled and squeezed Zanyr's fingers before reaching her other hand out to Torren. "That sounds like a good place to start."

She was right about that. This was a good beginning. The problem was, he already wanted more.

Patience. She wasn't Vardarian, so she would need more time to come to terms with the situation. He'd vowed to keep her safe and happy. That meant curbing his desires until she was ready.

Qarf. He hoped that didn't take long.

5

Jenna and her newly discovered mates talked about easy things, the way strangers do when they are first getting acquainted. Torren told stories about his family, mostly about the mischief he got into when one of his fathers first introduced him to chemistry.

Zanyr spoke about his work on the farm along with vivid descriptions of the land that made her long to see it for herself. In turn, she shared parts of her story—where she'd been raised and how she'd made a living for herself instead of signing on with the corporation that held the debt she'd incurred while living under their care.

Torren raised his hand. "Wait. You mean the corporation that raised you expected to be paid back for the cost of your upbringing?"

"It's the way it works." Jenna shrugged. To her, this was simply a fact of life. "They consider it an investment, and they expect to make a profit in the end. Usually, that means their wards sign employment contracts once they turn seventeen. They work for the corporation until their debt is paid off."

"How long does that usually take?" Zanyr asked. He leaned toward her as he spoke, his amber gaze fixed on her.

The attention made her uncomfortable, but she did her best to ignore the feeling as she answered his question.

"That depends on the type of work done. If someone has specialized skills or takes on high-risk jobs, they could clear their debt in about twenty years, sometimes less. For basic labor, it could take forty years or even more if they incur more debt for violations, additional training, or serious medical expenses."

"They penalize their employees for getting hurt or getting additional instruction?" Zanyr looked perplexed and horrified at the same time.

"Why hasn't your species done something to stop this?" Torren asked.

She'd asked the same question more than once, and the answer was always the same. "They do, Zanyr. And we can't stop it because somewhere in our history, we allowed the corporations to grow too powerful. We set ourselves on this path, and by the time we realized what was happening, it was already too late. They control most of the wealth, power, and influence, and no one can hold them accountable. Well, almost no one. The Interstellar Armed Forces, especially Nova Force, does what it can, but they have no jurisdiction over Earth or any corporate-owned planet."

The three of them lapsed into silence for a long

moment. Jenna picked at the food Saral had brought out, but nothing tasted as good as it had a few minutes ago.

"We need to bring more of your females here," Torren said.

Zanyr sighed and scrubbed a hand over his stubbled chin. "We're trying. I mean, the leadership council wants to do more, but we're being blocked at every turn. The corporations don't want to lose their pool of potential workers, plus many of them are still angry we were given this planet at all. They'd rather we packed up and went back to our part of the galaxy."

She'd forgotten Zanyr was on the leadership council. He didn't act or look anything like she'd expected. Though, now she thought about it, most of the council were surprisingly ordinary. Except for Prince Tyran, of course. He was a royal in every sense of the word. "You've done more than anyone else has. If not for the chance to come here, I would have spent the rest of my life on Earth."

"There's no other way out?" Torren asked.

Zanyr answered first. "Other ways, yes. Good ways? No. Earthers can buy their way onto a colonist ship and hope the place they land will support a colony. Some pay even more to try to reach one of the independent stations, but that's a big risk. From what I understand, more humans end up spaced, forcefully recruited into criminal groups, or sold into slavery than ever reach safety and freedom."

Then he cocked an eyebrow at his *anrik*. "I've mentioned this before. You should pay more attention to my venting after I come back from my meetings."

Torren held up both hands. "I try. But the important stuff must have gotten lost between your rants about a reliable food supply for the colony's livestock and the long-running argument over what kind of law enforcement this colony should have."

"It's *all* important," Zanyr grumbled.

"And I want to hear all about it. I mean, everything you're allowed to talk about," Jenna said.

She'd learned far more than her former employers realized because most of them didn't see the staff as people and spoke of all kinds of things where they could be overheard. She'd learned this skill after her first family kept secrets she should have been aware of, like the fact they never intended to take her with them when they left Earth for their next assignment. That betrayal left her with lasting scars and a vested interest in knowing what was really going on around her.

"You would?" Zanyr's expression softened into a pleased smile.

"Now that's an idea. Zan, you can vent to our *mahaya* from now on and leave me in peace!" Torren looked utterly smug as he made his suggestion.

"That's fine with me. There's so much I want to know about Haven and how it works. We've been told the basics, of course, but you've seen it all from a very different perspective." Her interest was real, but she had an ulterior motive. She could feed some of the most innocuous information to the ones who had recruited her. She'd need Shadow's help to figure out which items would be the least dangerous but would make it look like she was doing her part.

Unless, of course, the males she was now mated to were part of the plot. Then they'd know right away that she wasn't giving them anything useful because they'd already have far better information. *Fraxx.*

She was so not cut out for this spying thing.

Saral's prediction that they wouldn't stay too long proved accurate. Jenna didn't know how the two males were doing, but she was under constant bombardment by lurid thoughts and a near constant need for her *mahoyen.* It was distracting, and the gradual loss of control was alarming. She wasn't entirely in charge of her body or her mind at the moment, and from all reports, this was only the beginning. The *sharhal* would intensify over the next day or so, and there'd be no relief until they were fully bonded. Which meant sometime soon they'd move from talking to nakedness, sex, and biting.

The thought made her toes curl in anticipation. If sex with them was anything like the kisses they'd shared, she'd deal with the strangeness of going to bed with two males she barely knew.

Unsure what would happen next, she let them guide her out of the tavern and into the glorious sunshine. It was early autumn in the colony, with cooler nights and shorter days marking the end of her first summer.

Autumn, spring, summer, and winter were only words to her before coming to the colony. Nothing much grew outside the energy shields that protected her former home. Every season looked the same as any other from the inside. Though her employers lived on the upper levels, most of the hive's citizens lived in the cramped lower areas, far from the surface of their ruined planet.

One of the few perks of her profession was that she lived with or near the families employing her so she could be on hand to care for the children. That meant access to better food, clean water, and a chance to glimpse the sun from time to time. As weak and filtered as it was by pollution and the energy shield, it was still more than she'd have if she'd lived below ground.

It came as a surprise when Torren stopped and turned to look at her. "What would you like to do?"

"Me?" This might be the first time in her life someone had asked her that question. She'd assumed the meet-and-greet stage had ended and they'd be moving on to... whatever came next.

"Uh. Shouldn't we be, you know, getting on with things?" The moment the words were out of her mouth, she wished to all the stars she could take them back.

Torren grinned wickedly. "That's certainly one option. But if you aren't ready for that, we could do something else. You flew with me already. Would you like to fly with Zanyr? Maybe go see the ocean?"

She managed to stop herself from squealing with delight, but it was a near thing. "Could we?"

Zanyr looked at Torren, and the two exchanged a look she couldn't interpret.

"Ah," he said several seconds later. "Torren said you stared at the ocean on your way here. Have you never seen it before?"

"You noticed that?" She felt like all she was doing

was asking obvious questions, but her brain was not functioning well, and she hoped the males were distracted enough not to notice.

"I did. It reminded me I haven't flown to see it in ages. When we first came here, I flew to the shore every few days," Torren said. "Neither of us spent much time on planets in the last few years. Our miss—our work didn't allow for much down time."

"I know that feeling." Jenna caught the sudden change in wording but didn't comment, though she was curious about what he'd almost said instead. Something about their past? The work they did? They'd told her they worked security for freighting companies, guarding ships and their cargos from raiders and other dangers.

She realized that both of them were waiting for her to answer Zanyr's question and hurriedly framed a reply. "The closest I've come to an ocean was a sim-pod program I found on the journey out here. The day we landed, it rained so hard we didn't see much after entering the atmosphere. I did see it from orbit, though." She smiled at the memory. "We were all so excited. None of us had ever seen so much water."

"No one took you to see it since you arrived? I'd have thought the organizers would give you a chance to explore your new home a little." Zanyr frowned. "What were you doing all the time you were sequestered from the rest of the colony?"

"Learning how to live here," she said. "Remember that we had no experience with things you take for granted. I and the others lived our entire lives indoors. No weather, no wild flora, and no fauna to worry about.

Veth, it took time just to look up at the open sky without panicking. All this space." She let go of their hands, spread her arms, and raised them toward the blue sky. "It takes some getting used to. So did the higher gravity. The shots and conditioning on the ship here helped, but it was still tiring."

Torren winced. "Apologies, blossom. I didn't consider your situation before flying off with you. I hope you weren't distressed."

"I wasn't. If I'd had concerns, I would have said something. I'm shy. I know that. But I can speak up if I need to."

Zanyr smiled and reached for her. "That's good. We have a lot to learn about each other, and we're bound to make mistakes. Well, I am." He jerked his head toward Torren. "That one keeps telling me he's never wrong."

Torren drew himself to his full height, his mannerisms changing to that of an aloof aristocrat or a high-level corporate executive.

Looking down his nose at Zanyr, he drolled, "Your pitiful attempts to make me look bad in front of our *mahaya* are doomed to fail. She is our mate, and she will come to care for us both... which, in your case, is a testament to the power of the bond we share."

"Don't pull that courtly manner crap with me, you overbred *bakaffa*." Zanyr flicked a rude gesture in Torren's direction and then held the same hand out to her. "Come with me, *ana-thi*. We have an ocean to see."

"Why do you call me that? It means fair wind. Right?" She let him draw her in close before asking.

"That's what you are. A gift carried to us by the fairest of winds."

She considered that and then beamed. "I like it."

"See? She likes my name for her better than yours. Blossom is boring. You'll have to do better." Zanyr swept her into his arms and took off before Torren could answer, but she heard his laughter as they rose into the wide blue sky.

"I like blossom too!" she called out, hoping Torren heard her. She had no experience balancing the emotional needs of two males, but she guessed that having them compete for attention would never lead anywhere good.

6

Torren flew after his *anrik* and their mate, following only a few wingbeats behind them. As much as he disliked being parted from Jenna, he needed a few minutes alone. So much had happened today, and he'd been reacting to the situation with no chance to make a plan.

Life as a mercenary had taught him to always be prepared for the unexpected, and his role as a sometimes-assassin showed him that anyone was vulnerable. However, his easiest marks had been the ones who couldn't adapt when the wind changed. He prided himself on his ability to make a plan but change it on the fly. Finding Jenna meant adapting quickly, and to do that, he needed time to think.

Moving her to the farm wouldn't be an issue. They had more than enough space, and they'd made the decision to furnish the largest bedroom with a bed, dresser, and other basics. Jenna could decorate it however she wished, but at least they could show her that they had planned for the day they found their mate.

Transport would be an issue. They'd need to acquire a land vehicle Jenna could drive into Haven and back. The farm was too far from the colony to walk easily, and she couldn't fly. It would be strange to have a mate without wings. They'd have to adjust some things, but nothing of real import. If she wanted to learn, they could look into buying a small aircraft of some kind. Surely the humans had that kind of thing? Then she could fly with them.

By the time they reached the shores of the ocean, he'd used his com to record two separate lists. One was a series of questions for Jenna. Her likes and dislikes, preferred foods, and a host of other details. The other was for him and Zanyr and itemized all the things they'd want to consider and then address to make their place welcoming for their *mahaya*.

At the top of that list were two things they needed to do quickly—select a blade to gift to their mate and commission a set of armbands for all three of them to signify their new status. He knew several artisans who could do the work, but Damos and his *anrik* Tra'var were the best forgemasters in the colony, and Jenna deserved the best of everything.

It was a simple, straightforward set of plans. The hard part would be figuring out how to tell her that she was mated to a pair of former mercenaries with a past strewn with bodies, blood, and brutality.

He landed and watched as Jenna kicked off her shoes and ran toward the water. Her laughter danced on the ocean breeze as she raced across the sand. She yelped as the first wave washed over her feet, nearly leaping into the air with surprise.

"It's warm!"

"The sun has warmed the sand, which heats the water as the tide comes in. Further out it cools off quickly." He'd discovered that fact for himself the first time he'd swum out to deeper water.

So far, the biologists hadn't found anything in the local waters that posed a threat to the colonists, but they still had more to learn about the currents and tides. The ocean, like everything else on this planet, was relatively unexplored and full of mysteries.

Jenna seemed aware of this because she didn't go in past her ankles. She seemed content to wade in the shallows with her skirt in one hand to keep it out of the water. She picked up shells, rocks, and anything else that caught her eye, but she placed everything back where she'd found it.

Struck with inspiration, he sent a message to Zanyr, and they both set to work looking for some small treasure for her to take back as a memento of the day.

"You think there are any gemstones here? Or are we going to wind up giving her something as mundane as a stone?" Zanyr asked via their link.

"If you manage to find a qarfing *gem on the beach, we'll get it polished and set into a* harani *for our mate. But I'm pretty sure that's not how mining works."*

"You found our mahaya *on your way to work. If we were ever going to get that lucky, today would be the day."*

They finished their impromptu treasure hunt not

long before Jenna retreated from the water's edge. Her dress was damp, her hair disheveled from the wind. Her smile made him wish he had the cyborg's ability to capture a memory and record it forever.

She looked relaxed, happy. Beautiful... and may the ancestors give him strength, utterly fuckable.

Only it was too soon. Too quick. They had to give her time, no matter how much he ached to be inside her.

His balls tightened and his cock twitched in his pants. Turning away from her, he tried to adjust himself, but the discomfort continued.

Zanyr's laughter buzzed inside his head, but the *bakaffa* was suffering as much as he was.

"Cold shower before bed tonight?" He sent back to Zanyr. It was something he'd heard the cyborg males joke about. It sounded barbaric, but maybe it would help them get through the night.

The *sharhal* would only intensify as time passed, though it was worse when he was in her company. It was the same for Zanyr. The blending of their blood was more than a symbol of their bond. It linked their nanotech and altered their bodies' chemistry, greatly increasing the odds that they'd bond to the same female.

It would be a long night for them both. Possibly for Jenna, too, but he couldn't be sure how the mating fever would affect her. He didn't dare ask, either. He'd seen the way Jenna reacted to Saral's comments earlier. Humans weren't as open about sex as his race. At least, that's how it seemed to him.

Jenna called to them, her smile still brighter than the

afternoon sun. "Can we come back here sometime? Maybe have a picnic? It's wonderful!"

"Of course," Zanyr replied. "Anywhere you want to go, we'll take you."

"You mean, anywhere on the planet," she corrected him gently. "You are allowed to leave, but I'm not. At least, I won't be once I accept the medi-bot treatment."

Zanyr scowled and cracked the knuckles of his right hand. "As our mate, you'll go where we go."

"Zan is right about that. And remember, you won't receive the medi-bot treatment created by humans. Once we claim you, you'll carry both of *our* nanotech. That technology is outside your government's purview. You'll be free to travel anywhere you wish."

He smiled as her eyes widened in sudden understanding.

"I forgot about that." She touched her temple with two fingers. "My brain is all jumbled right now. Especially when I think about how that transfer is done. Biting during... um..." she gestured at herself and then at the two of them. "During mating."

Mating. The word rang in his ears and sent half the blood in his body flooding straight to his cock. He wanted that. Wanted to bury himself in her body and hear her soft little gasps and groans as he showed her what it really meant to be mated.

"Yes, blossom. That's when we'll claim you." Zanyr's voice was dark and tight with what Zanyr realized was arousal. If they kept talking about it, they'd wind up doing more than just talking.

Zanyr had moved closer to Jenna, and his scales had

tightened to a shimmering gold he'd didn't often see when they weren't in combat. Yeah, his *anrik* was deep in the thrall of the *sharhal*.

The wind shifted direction as they spoke. It flowed in from offshore, brisk, cool, and heavy with the scent of rain. He glanced up and noted the dark clouds blotting out the horizon. *Veth*. When had that happened?

"Storm coming," he sent to Zanyr. It was only an observation, but the words held a note of foreboding he didn't understand.

It was a change in the weather. Nothing more. Unlike many soldiers he'd known, Torren wasn't superstitious. He didn't believe in omens or rituals. He'd known males who never changed their socks before a battle, or always carried a talisman with them for luck.

If the universe worked that way, he'd never seen any sign of it. The ancestors were another matter. They didn't provide guidance or protection. They simply watched, judged, and sometimes sent signs when they approved or were displeased. They didn't interfere in the lives of their descendants or the choices they made.

At least, that's what Torren believed. Others held different views, but that was also their choice. In the end, that's all any of them had—the right to choose for themselves. That was why he'd left home in the first place, and Zanyr had done the same.

Zanyr turned to look over his shoulder and then grunted in annoyance. "Looks like your first visit to the beach is over. We should get back to Haven before the rain starts."

As if to underscore his words, the wind gusted hard

enough to make all three of them shiver at the sudden drop in temperature.

"Is that why it's colder now?" She wrapped her arms around her upper body. Torren registered the gesture and then realized the cause. Their *mahaya* wasn't dressed for flying. Her simple navy-blue dress was too light to offer her any protection from the elements, and she didn't have any nanotech to help her regulate her body temperature.

Zanyr was bare-chested, and all Torren had to offer her was the sleeveless vest he wore. Still, it was something. He skinned it over his head and handed it to her.

"Put this on. It should help keep you warm on the flight back."

She blinked at him, ignoring the offered garment to stare at him. "You're half naked."

"Only half," he joked. "Now I match Zan, who was in such a hurry to meet you he forgot how to dress himself."

Zanyr scoffed and slapped his palm to his chest. "I had my priorities straight."

"I've never been anyone's priority before. Thank you." Jenna's words hit with all the force of a comet strike.

Without thinking about what he was doing, Torren stepped in front of her and dropped to one knee, the simple treasure he'd found for her resting on his upturned palm. "You will *always* be our priority, Jenna."

Zanyr knelt to his left and made his offering a split-second later. "Witnessed."

"I... uh... wow," Jenna stammered. She reached for

them uncertainly, her hands shaking as they hovered in the air without making contact with either male.

"We are yours, *mahaya*, and you are ours. As strange as this may be to you, it is the truth," Zanyr said, his voice soft and melodic. Torren didn't see this side of his *anrik* often. The male had the mind and body of a warrior, but he had the heart of a poet.

She carefully took the offered gifts from their hands. "These are for me?"

"Reminders of our first day together." Zanyr pointed to the bit of driftwood he'd given her. "The sea has caressed this wood so often it's been polished smooth. That's what I want for us, *ana-thi*—a lifetime of love and caresses that leave us both polished and shining."

Jenna's eyes lit up as her fingers closed around the driftwood. "That's beautiful, Zanyr. I-I don't know what to say." She laughed. "I know dozens of languages, but I don't have the words for what I'm feeling right now. So, thank you, my *mahoyen*." She spoke the words in Vardarian and then again in Galactic Common. "Thank you for your beautiful words. I won't ever forget them."

Torren inwardly cursed his friend in every language he knew. By all the winds that blew, how was he supposed to follow *that*?

He waited for inspiration to strike, but nothing came to him. Aware that he had to say something, Torren went with the simple truth. He touched the seashell she held in one hand. "I chose this because the color reminded me of the sky, and the way the shell twists and whirls made me think of the wind as it swirled around us on our first flight."

Zanyr stayed outwardly silent, but he sent a message to Torren. *"Not bad, Vex. Your time at court is showing."*

"Fraxx off." He sent the message without looking at his *anrik*. He knew the smug male would be trying to hide a smirk but probably failing at it.

Jenna looked up at him with soft brown eyes. "I will treasure the memory of that first flight forever. You showed me Haven from a new perspective, all from the safety of your arms."

"And we'll fly again soon. Very soon, in fact. Come here, Jenna. It's time we took you home."

Zanyr nodded. "I'll fly cover. But first, I need to kiss our mate again."

Watching his *anrik* sweep their mate into his arms was something he'd imagined hundreds of times, but the reality was far more satisfying. She smiled and went to Zanyr with a shy eagerness that melted Torren's heart. A sense of tenderness coupled with a powerful urge to nurture and protect his mate bloomed like a flame in the darkest hour of the night.

So this was the *sharhal*. No one had warned him that the sudden rush of desire wasn't the strangest or the strongest element of the mating fever. It was the sense of soaring on an unseen wind so powerful he couldn't break free. All he could do was hang on and see where it took him.

He watched and waited for Jenna to finish her kiss with Zanyr before she returned to his side. Wherever this wind would take him, they'd make the journey together.

7

Flying in the rain wasn't nearly as much fun as she'd hoped. In fact, it sucked harder than a black hole. The weather caught up to them long before they made it back to Haven, drenching all three of them. Water streamed down her face, half-blinding her. She quickly gave up trying to see anything and buried her face in the crook of Torren's shoulder to avoid the worst of the wind.

Zanyr flew above and slightly ahead of them, so close it seemed as if she could reach out and touch him. Flying cover, he'd called it. She'd wondered what that meant, and now she knew. He was using his body to shield them from the weather.

When they neared the colony, Torren squeezed her shoulders to get her attention.

"Where?" he asked, his voice raised to be heard over the wind.

She wiped a fresh spray of rain from her eyes and looked around, trying to get her bearings from this new vantage point. It took her longer than she liked to find a landmark she recognized, but eventually she found her house.

"There." She pointed. "The one with the diamond on the roof."

That's when she noticed that every home had a different design, clearly visible from the air. It made sense, but it was one more detail she hadn't known about her new home. There was so much she needed to learn.

She thought they'd land on the roof, but they landed on the street near the gate to her home. As they touched down, one of her neighbors paused at their window to scowl at them. Jenna flinched, surprised by the hostility in the female's expression. Tani hadn't been overly friendly in the short time she'd lived here, but now she looked furious... and disgusted.

Torren growled, pivoting as he spread his wings to shield her from Tani's glare. "Ignore her."

"She's my neighbor. Ignoring her isn't going to be easy. Do you think this will happen often?" She knew about the *Liq'za*. They'd been briefed more than once on the faction of Vardarian society who believed that their species was superior to all others. They advocated for traditional values and racial purity. Haven colony was founded to escape those concepts, but somehow the ideas had made their way here, and lately, they seemed to have taken root.

No one knew how it had happened or who was behind the infiltration, but Jenna had heard the gossip. Some said it was Prince Tyran's sister, Empress Neha, who was still stung that her brother had broken away to start his own colony. Others whispered that it was not

Neha but a rogue faction of her court who were trying to destroy the colony before others decided to follow suit. Jenna had read enough history, both Vardarian and human, to come up with her own theory. She didn't think the *Liq'za* had any long-term goals or a proper agenda. Some would be like-minded; others would only agree in the broadest of terms. Anger was the fuel that kept the fire burning, and fear fanned the flames.

"It won't happen at all. Not if I have anything to say about it," Zanyr stated, his words edged with ice. He turned to face Tani's house and then raised his voice loudly enough to be sure she and everyone else around heard. "As it happens, I'm part of the leadership council, so I *do* have a say. It's time to send a message to these beings. Haven was founded to be a place of acceptance and community. If they don't value those things, they are free to leave. Immediately."

Torren leaned down to nuzzle her hair as he whispered, "Zan tends to be dramatic sometimes, but he means every word. Your neighbor has been warned. If she gives you so much as a sideways glance, you tell us and we'll handle it."

She leaned into Torren and nodded once. "I doubt she'll do anything else. I'm sorry she feels that way, though. I don't understand why someone would join the colony if they didn't want to be around other species."

"Neither do I, blossom. We need to remind everyone that we came here to make a fresh start, somewhere that everyone is welcome."

"Hopefully they'll remember. But what if they don't?"

"Bluster and dramatic poses aside, Zanyr is right. If they can't accept the way things are done here, they need to leave."

The idea didn't give her a good feeling, but neither did knowing she lived beside someone who disapproved of her for no good reason.

Zanyr must have sensed her thoughts because he took her hand and squeezed it gently. "Sometimes a farmer has to cut away a blighted part of a plant to save it. If they don't intervene, the rot will work its way to the root. Haven's still a young colony. If we don't take care of it now, it won't thrive the way it could have."

"I know, and I get it. But couldn't Tani and the ones who think like her say the same thing?"

"They could." Zanyr scowled. "Hell, they probably do, but only among themselves. If they had legitimate concerns about something, they could bring them to the council or advocate for change. No one has done that. They just whisper to each other in the shadows. Nothing good can grow in those conditions."

Torren chuckled and shook his wings hard enough to splatter Zanyr with water. "Agricultural metaphors. Really? That's the best you could do?"

"It's what I know. Nothing is stopping you from spouting some chemistry-based wisdom."

"My good sense is stopping me. That and a desire to get out of this weather."

"I second that last bit. I am soaked to the skin. If I'm going to fly with you often, I'll need to expand my wardrobe."

"I'm sure the shops will have something appropriate,"

Torren said. He let go of her, and she walked over to the gate, unlocked it, and gestured for them to follow her inside.

Zanyr fell in behind her. "First, we'll shop for something appropriate. Then I think we should buy our *mahaya* a few things that are definitely *not* appropriate. I have heard others talk about something called lingerie. I am intrigued."

Torren groaned and threw up his hands. "Apologies, Jenna. Despite my best efforts, Zan is not always fit for decent company."

She laughed. "I don't care about that. Before I came here, I made a living raising and teaching the next generation of corporate executives. The first thing those children are taught is to conform to expectations. Even if it means lying to themselves and everyone else. The second thing they learn is how to use language as a weapon, especially polite language. I'd much rather both of you speak bluntly rather than play word games."

Once she got the door unlocked, she pushed it open and stepped inside. "Welcome to my home. I'm afraid there's not much to it. I haven't been her long enough to decorate. Oh, and Zan?" She used the nickname Torren had used several times today.

"Yes?"

"I've never owned lingerie before, but I'm not averse to modeling some for you... if we can find any."

"We'll find some," Zanyr declared immediately. "Even if we have to pay Hezza to import it."

"Oh! Hezza. Of course." She'd forgotten about the gregarious freighter pilot who had often visited their camp and brought them all sorts of things from other parts of the galaxy. While most traders were restricted to the orbital platform these days, Hezza was a trusted member of the community, even if she was only here part of the time. It didn't hurt that she was Anya's mother. They were both committed to the success of the colony and their own business ventures.

"We'll talk about what you need to buy soon. Right now, you need to get yourself dry and warm," Torren said.

Jenna glanced down at the floor, which now had three slowly growing pools of water where each of them stood. "I'll do that. Help yourself to towels to dry off. You'll find plenty in the closet right there." She pointed to a spot not far from where they were standing. "And don't worry about the floor. The bots will handle it."

She'd been shocked to discover her home, which had been gifted to her once she'd been granted full citizenship in the colony, came with comfortable furniture, a food dispenser, and small household droids that did most of the housework and maintenance. Even when she'd been contracted to live with the families she worked for and had been surrounded by luxury, her room had always been small, shabby, and equipped with only the barest of essentials.

"Sorry to leave you alone for a bit. I won't be long." It felt odd to just leave the two of them downstairs, but if she invited them up to her room, that would only end one way. So far, they hadn't pushed her for more than some scorching hot kisses. Were they waiting to give her time? Or were they unsure that this was what they wanted.

That *she* was what they wanted. A little period of adjustment would be best for all of them. Wouldn't it?

As she climbed the stairs to the second floor, she had to squelch the temptation to call down to them and ask them to join her. She managed to reach her room, but deep inside, she knew she wouldn't be able to resist the *sharhal* much longer.

It took more willpower than Zanyr wanted to admit for him to resist the urge to follow Jenna upstairs. He didn't want to let her out of his sight.

"I know," Torren nodded toward the stairs. "Believe me, I don't want to be separated from her either, but we have to let her be. She needs time." He pointed to the kitchen and lowered his voice so they wouldn't be overheard. "And we need to talk."

"About what? And why aren't we using the link?" Zan asked.

"If you had two unexpected guests downstairs, would you feel comfortable if they lapsed into total silence?"

"Fair point. I'd wonder what the *qarf* they were up to and come down to check on them."

"Exactly. This way we're making a reasonable amount of noise, but she won't be able to make out anything we say."

"And you don't want her to hear us?" Zan looked around the kitchen area, taking note of everything he saw. She really hadn't been here long. No scuffs or scratches on the walls or the floor, and the counters were immaculate, as if she'd not dared to set anything down on them yet.

"I don't." Torren had the cooling unit open and was checking out the contents. Apart from several containers of fruit juice and a takeout box from one of the local eateries, it was empty.

"So, we're having *that* conversation. Are we going for the long and wordy version, or can we cut this down to a simple yes or no?"

"This is important, Zan. I think we owe it to her to have a real discussion about it." At some point Torren had drawn his dagger from his belt and was flipping it between his fingers. The old habit usually meant he was agitated or thinking hard. In this case, Zanyr figured it was a bit of both.

"So, long and wordy it is. You want to talk first, or shall I?"

Torren pointed at him. "You start. I'll see if there's anything in the food dispenser to give to our mate to help warm her up faster."

"Try not to poison her," Zan goaded his *anrik* and then spent a few seconds organizing his thoughts. "*Sharhal* aside, I like her. She's funny, sweet, and clearly smart. Probably smarter than either of us."

Torren snorted. "Smarter than you, yes. Me? Maybe."

Zanyr ignored the jibe. "The thing is, she's gentle. You've seen that. Right?"

"I have." Torren kept scanning the menu on the dispenser while they talked. "Your point?"

"What is she going to think when we tell her who we were? What we did? My own family can't deal with it.

The only communication I have with them are written messages. What if she can't accept us? What happens then?" They'd both heard stories about failed matings. They rarely ended well for anyone involved. At best, those involved were left with heartbreak and emotional scars. At worst... He didn't want to think about that.

Torren made a selection and watched to ensure the program started before turning to look at him. "You want to lie to her for the rest of our lives? That won't work. She'll figure out we're hiding something from her."

"Yes. But not right away. I don't want to lie to her forever." Zanyr scrubbed a hand through his hair in frustration. "But I want her to get a chance to know who we are now before we tell her who and what we used to be."

He tensed, expecting Torren to argue with him. To his surprise, his *anrik* only nodded. "I agree. We should wait a while before we have that conversation. A few days won't do any harm." He reached toward him, his fist closed and his scar visible. "We tell her soon, but not yet. She's our *mahaya*, and she deserves to know the truth."

He sheathed his dagger and held out his hand. They crossed wrists, their scars touching. Zanyr could still remember the day they'd cut themselves and performed the bonding ritual. It felt like a lifetime ago.

"We've come a long way together, my brother."

"We have. And we *found* her." Torren looked dazed for a moment. "I wondered if we ever would."

Zanyr tapped his chest. "You had doubts. Me? I was always sure we'd find our mate. I mean, we're good-looking, smart, and charming. Oh, wait. I'm all those things. You're... sorry, Vex, but let's be honest here. You're just you."

"Asshole."

"But you said it with love."

At that moment, the dispenser gurgled, burped, and spat a generous quantity of something hot, thick, and beige into the waiting bowl. "What is *that?*"

"Something called porr-idge." Torren sounded out the strange word. "My translator is having trouble finding a match for it in our language."

"I'm having trouble believing that's edible." Zanyr took the bowl out of the dispenser and sniffed it suspiciously. "It has about as much scent as it does color. As in, almost none." He set the bowl down before it burned his fingers. "This is food. You're sure?"

"It was on the menu, so yes, I'm sure it's food. It was listed under breakfast and marked as a favorite item. Whatever it is, Jenna must like it."

"You should taste it."

Torren shot him a look of disbelief. "You sniffed it already. You try it."

"You decided to make it."

After a few more seconds of staring, Torren found two spoons and handed one to Zanyr. "Together."

After swallowing, Zanyr shook his head. "Apparently porridge means 'has no discernable flavor, texture, or smell.' What else does she have listed under favorites? That can't be it."

It wasn't. Jenna had several other meals tagged. They were familiar with several of them from eating at the Bar None and another restaurant called Earthly Delights.

Curious, they selected another one neither they nor their translation program had heard of.

The second he caught a whiff of the newly prepared meal, Zanyr dug in. "Tamales are much better than porridge. You have to try this." He took another spoonful before Torren managed even one.

"This is much better. We'll have to ask her what ingredients the dispenser needs to make it at home."

Zanyr was already perusing the menu, looking for something else to try. "It's good, but do you think it's what she'll want to eat? She's already had two meals today. Oh, here's something. Chicken soup. I know what chickens are, and soup is a lighter meal."

"And we've devoured half the tamale dish already. Better make her something else."

The soup wasn't what they'd expected. Instead of a simple broth, it was made with a medley of vegetables and bite-sized lumps of dough they decided were dumplings. It looked so good they ate it with the rest of the tamales. "We don't know how long she'll be, and we wouldn't want it to get cold."

"Definitely not."

8

———

Since she was already soaking wet, Jenna decided she might as well take a quick shower. She hadn't gotten all the sand off her feet before putting her shoes back on as they hurried to leave the beach, and her lower legs itched from the salt water. She wasn't cleaning up so she could look her best for the males downstairs. Not at all. This was entirely a practical decision.

"And when you wake up tomorrow, you'll have wings and a tail," she muttered to herself. Actually, wings would be nice. Then she'd at least be able to fly with her mates and not be a burden they had to carry around from place to place.

She hated the idea of being a problem someone had to deal with. She'd grown up hearing that, as if it was somehow her fault that her parents were dead. That's why she'd taken that first job offer, though at the time it had been couched as something else. Juveniles weren't supposed to work until they turned seventeen. It was one of the few laws the corporations obeyed for the most part.

That first assignment had been an "opportunity." The Andersons had recently been transferred to the city and had discovered that very few children were a match in age among the other executives living there. That's when they'd approached the care center and made an offer. They wanted a companion for their daughter and agreed to take over the feeding, care, and education of that companion for a set period.

At the time, she'd been thrilled to be selected. She was too young to understand that she wasn't a new addition to the family, and so was Rani, their daughter. They declared themselves sisters and did everything together, despite the fact Jenna was two years her senior.

Three years later, the Andersons announced they'd been transferred to a new station. The family packed up their belongings. Jenna had helped Rani pack, and then the girl she thought of as family had helped her do the same. As far as they knew, Jenna was coming with them. She was part of the family, after all.

Only it turned out she wasn't.

Rani had burst through the door into her room, interrupting Jenna's evening meal. The first words out of her mouth sent Jenna's world crashing down around her.

"You're not coming with us."

They only had a few minutes to say goodbye to each other before someone from the care center arrived to collect her. They'd spent those bitter moments crying, hugging, and making countless promises they'd never be able to keep. To visit. To write. To send vid messages every day.

She never got to talk to the Anderson adults. She had

no chance to ask them why they weren't taking her. Hadn't she been good enough? Smart enough? Had she eaten too much food or not helped Rani enough with her schoolwork?

"Enough." Jenna slapped at the water controls with enough force to sting her hand. She wasn't that girl anymore, and this wasn't Earth. What point was there in delving into memories of her time there? Especially those memories.

The answer was obvious. She was afraid the past was about to repeat itself. Torren and Zanyr were gorgeous, well-respected pillars of this community. She was a newcomer with no standing and a job she hadn't even started yet. No wonder Tani had looked at her that way. She was an interloper, waltzing in to take things she had no right to.

"Stop it." She gave herself a mental shake and followed it up with a light slap to the back of her hand. She had to think of something else—something bright and happy so the voices of doubt would shut up and leave her alone. If she didn't, they'd drag her down into a dark place and leave her there to twist herself into knots.

She activated the drying cycle and let the hot air work its magic. It was another luxury she'd never expected to enjoy, something meant for the special few who deserved the best of everything.

Why them? She'd asked that question so often, but she'd never finished the thought. Today, she did. Why them but not me?

No answer came to her, not even the negative voices responding. She spoke aloud this time, the words weighted as they rolled off her tongue. "Why not me?" Then she answered her own question, throwing out all the harsh things she'd told herself over the years. "Because I'm not good enough. I'm not pretty enough. I'm not anything special."

Jenna sucked in a deep breath. "But I don't believe that. I won't." Another breath. "I can't. I deserve to be happy, dammit."

Even as she made her breakthrough statement, she hoped to the stars above that neither male could hear her right now. One day, maybe, she'd tell them about her self-doubts. Right after she figured out how to tell them she was a spy.

Veth! The moment of truth and introspection ended so quickly she felt a little unsteady, but she hurried out of the bathroom before the dry cycle had finished. She needed to send a message to her Vardarian contact.

"Because I didn't have enough to deal with already today," she muttered.

It took several attempts to craft a message she was happy with. In the end, she stuck to the basics and deleted everything else.

Have met two Vardarian males, Torren Vex and Zanyr Sallesh. Am experiencing sharhal symptoms. Please advise.

She sent it to Shadow via a heavily encoded device she'd been given. She kept it hidden in her bedroom closet, tucked into the pocket of an old sweater she'd brought with her from Earth.

She wouldn't contact the other group until she heard back from Shadow. She had another encoded comm for *them*. She'd returned to her habi-pod one day after classes and found a parcel by her door. Inside was the comm and instructions on how and when to use it as well as where to hide it the rest of the time. She thought it must have been the other spy in their class—Reni. But that left the question of where she had gotten the comm from.

Jenna had wanted to ask about that, but it wasn't her job to ask questions. All she had to do was go about her life, report any contact from the enemy, and forward whatever false information Shadow provided her.

Almost all her contact was via the encrypted comm. In-person meetings were rare and potentially risky, but in this case, she figured it would be necessary. They needed to brainstorm the best way to handle this unexpected twist in a way that benefited the colony and kept up the appearance of compliance with the enemy's directives.

She thought of them as the enemy because she didn't have any other name. The ones who recruited her had claimed to be a group of "concerned individuals." The Vardarians suspected they were part of something called the Shadow Men.

Once the message was sent and her comm hidden in the back of the closet once more, Jenna hurried to get dressed. She'd left her guests too long already.

Apparently, she'd left them on their own long enough for them to get hungry. That much was obvious the moment she opened her bedroom door and was assailed by the scent of cooking, but she wasn't sure just what she smelled. It was like several meals all jumbled together.

One look at her kitchen, and she understood why she hadn't recognized the scent. Judging by the dirty dishes, her mates had enjoyed a number of meals. She burst out laughing at the sight, not of the dishes, but of the almost identical expressions of guilt on both Zanyr's and Torren's faces.

"We wanted to make you something to eat," Torren explained.

"But Torren's first pick was the blandest thing I've ever tasted. So we had to try again."

"And that was good, but it didn't seem like the right meal for you."

"So we tried again."

She stood, bemused, as the two males finished each other's sentences. It made her wonder if their ability to work together seamlessly carried over to other skills. That, in turn, sent her brain down a wormhole of increasingly vivid, arousing images that almost derailed her thought process entirely. Whoa. She reined in her libido and managed to rejoin the conversation without it being too obvious what had happened. At least, she hoped so.

"I see. Which one did you decide on?"

"The soup," both of them answered at the same time.

"Oh! Good choice. Chicken and dumpling soup is my one of my favorites." She looked over the dishes and frowned. "Wait, these are all my favorites. How many did you try?"

"Three, Zanyr said, stepping to one side to block her view of a plate with several brownies on it.

"Four," Torren said.

"Well, four total. Three entrees and one dessert," Zanyr admitted. Then he brightened as he grabbed for the plate of brownies and offered it to her. "But we saved you some."

"Soup and brownies sound perfect. Thank you."

"You sit down. We'll bring it to you," Torren said.

"Right. Bringing it to you now." Zanyr set down the brownies in the middle of the table while she got seated. Torren delivered the soup, and then they made more tamales for themselves and brought them over to join her.

She was hungrier than she'd expected. It hadn't been that long since the meal at the tavern, but she polished off the soup and moved on to the brownies faster than normal. "I don't know why I'm so hungry. Maybe all the fresh air?"

Torren and Zanyr shared a knowing look. "It's probably the same reason we started eating your food without so much as asking permission," Torren said. "Sorry about that."

"The *sharhal* can affect a variety of things. I mean, other than the obvious." Zanyr grinned at her. "It can mess with your concentration, your need for sleep, and in some cases, accelerate the body's metabolism. I'd say we're experiencing at least some of those already."

"And it will only get worse?" Jenna winced. "Strike that. Bad wording. Not worse, stronger. We're going to be a mess in a day or so. Right?"

"That depends," Torren said.

"On what?" she asked.

The energy in the room changed, intensifying. Every second stretched out longer than it should have as a thrill of anticipation and hope raced through her.

"How long you want us to wait before we claim you," Zanyr said.

She turned her head to look at him and found herself captured in the brilliant amber fire of his eyes. For a moment, she thought she might go up in flames from the heat burning in his gaze, but she managed to focus on what he said.

They were leaving the choice up to her. These two proud males would fight the mating fever to give her time. It was gratifying. Flattering. Intoxicating to have that power over them both.

"I know what happens if we wait too long. I'll suffer, but not as badly as the two of you." She shook her head hard. "I don't want that. For you to suffer, I mean."

Jenna pushed back her chair and rose from the table. Her heart pounded against her ribs and her legs weren't entirely steady, but she managed to hold out a hand to each of them. "Today has been a day full of firsts. I think it's time for another."

"First?" Torren took her hand, but his tone was confused.

Zanyr chuckled and caught her hand in his large, callused one. "*Mahaya*, are you saying you've never been with two males before?"

She nodded, her mouth too dry for her to form words.

"Blessed winds," Torren breathed. "Truly?"

She nodded again.

"Then it's time to take you upstairs and show you what it means to have two mates. I promise you will enjoy every second," Torren said.

"Witnessed," Zanyr said.

Every word, every action, almost sizzled with desire. Jenna quivered, her body reacting no longer entirely under her control. Lust burned in her veins. Her skin was on fire, and every part of her ached for her males.

"Witnessed," she whispered.

"Good." Torren raised her hand to his mouth, his lips tracing paths of pleasure across her flesh. "Now, blossom. Show us the way to your bedroom."

9

For once, Zanyr was happy to follow someone else's lead. Especially if that someone was his mate, and she was taking him to the bedroom. Though by this point, he'd happily take her on any available surface. He'd never been this eager, this *hungry*, for a female before.

The need for her had been with him from the moment he first caught her scent, but it was intensifying. How had the prince and his consort managed to give their mate the time she needed to accept them? Phaedra was the first human female ever to bond with one of their kind, and the rumors claimed she made them wait two *days* before accepting them.

He didn't want to wait two more minutes, never mind two days.

The home she'd been assigned was based on one of the standard templates—machine-made, sturdy, and quick to build. They were typical Vardarian designs with open spaces that allowed the occupants to stretch their wings and even fly from place to place through the wide halls, broad doorways, and tall ceilings. Still, compared to their home out on the farm, it was relatively small.

The door to her bedroom was open, and the air still held traces of soap and steam from her recent shower. He let her go first and then grinned at his *anrik* and tried to elbow him out of the way so he could go in next. Torren blocked him with one wing and stepped neatly around his outstretched foot to slip past him with the grace of a dancer.

"Nice try," Torren sent.

Zanyr was too busy looking around the room to answer. Everything here was basic, functional, and probably had come with the house. A handful of photos sat in frames on top of a dresser, and the small treasures he and Torren had given her earlier took pride of place on an otherwise empty bedside table.

The bed was made up with simple, cream-colored sheets and a fluffy white coverlet. To his relief, he noted that the bed was also a standard Vardarian design and was made for more than one person. While it wasn't one of the larger styles, it would accommodate them all.

"Uh, so, this is it. My bed. I mean my bedroom. The main bathroom is that way." She pointed out the door and then gestured down the hall. "And the ensuite is there."

The door to her private bathing area was open, allowing him a view of cream and white fixtures that looked about as warm and inviting as a midnight swim during a blizzard. He'd spent too much of his life in rooms like this, though they'd never been this clean or new. Cold. Impersonal. As if whoever lived here knew they weren't going to stay, so why bother trying to make it a home.

He knew why he'd lived that way before coming to Haven. The question was why did Jenna?

Torren only had eyes for their *mahaya*. He prowled across the room like a predator stalking his prey, and Zanyr knew what would happen next. Torren Vex loved the chase more than any other male he'd ever met. Now they'd had her permission, it was time to play.

"We will never harm you, Jenna. Anything we do to you will be to bring you pleasure, not pain."

"Uh. Yes. Of course," Jenna said, but she took a step back at the same time, and her gaze dropped to the floor.

"Do not run from me." The words were silken, but a blade of pure steel lay hidden beneath them.

Jenna froze. "I'm not running." Her voice was softer than a whisper.

Zanyr watched, curious to see what Jenna did next. They had to figure out what she needed and what she was willing to accept.

"Do not hide from me either," Torren said.

"What do you want from me?" she asked without raising her voice or her eyes.

"Everything you're willing to give us. Your body. Your pleasure. Your trust." Torren reached out to her, his hand brushing her cheek. "And someday, when we've proven ourselves to you, I hope you'll give us one more thing."

She trembled, but neither male spoke. If she needed them to explain, they would, but what a gift it would be if she instinctively knew what they wanted.

"You..." she broke off. Her teeth sank into her lower lip for several seconds, and then she raised her head to look at them. *Both* of them. "You want me to submit to you."

It wasn't a question. Blessed ancestors, she *did* understand. It was enough. At least for now.

"We do," Zanyr joined the conversation. "But not until you are ready. That's a gift not easily given."

Her next breath came out in a soft huff that might have been laughter but was probably relief. "True. Thank you for giving me time."

Her lips thinned for a moment, and she moved her hands together in front of her, one hand rubbing the back of the other. "I know you'll both need time too. I mean, I'm not exactly what you were expecting. The females of your species are beautiful, strong, and well..." She shrugged both shoulders. "A lot taller than I am. They can fly, too."

Zanyr heard what she said, but the doubt in her voice drove daggers into his heart. She had doubts, not about them, but about herself.

"No," he said, the denial out of his mouth before his brain could catch up. When he couldn't think of what to say next, he let his heart do the talking. "You are not what we expected, *ana-thi*. You are so much more. I've done things in my life that I'm not proud of. Things that made me question if I would ever find my mate or have any of the things I truly wanted."

He closed the distance between them, stopping about a meter away. "Today, I got the answer to my questions. Today, the ancestors gifted me with you."

This wasn't what he'd intended. They should be in bed already, but something told him to hold tightly to his last shreds of control and do this right, even if he wasn't sure what that was.

"You really believe that?" Jenna asked.

"I do."

"As do I," Torren added. "You are our *mahaya*. The female we have been waiting for. A moment ago, I told you what we wanted from you. I want to know what you want from us."

Jenna sucked in a breath. "What I want?"

Both of them waited for her to continue, but she stayed silent.

"What do you wish for in the darkest hours of the night?" Zanyr prompted.

"There was a time I was alone in the galaxy. Shunned by my family and forgotten by everyone. Back then, I wished for a brother, a companion to laugh with, a warrior I could trust to have my back." Torren bowed his head toward Zanyr. "The ancestors led me to Zan, and we forged a bond that will last all our lives."

"Now, we want you to be part of that bond. As powerful as it is, it's still incomplete. We've been waiting for you, Jenna. Tell us what you need, what you dream of, so we can find a way to complete you, too."

Tears glittered in her eyes and spilled down her cheeks as Jenna looked at them. "I..." She blew out a breath and then started again. "I've never let myself think about things like that. It was easier to be content with what I had. I told you I was an orphan, but there's more to the story, and I don't want to tell it right now." She smiled softly. "I'd rather be doing other things."

"And we will get to them. Soon," Torren said. "But first, I want to know what you want from us."

"Okay. I can do that. Be honest with me. I know we all have secrets to protect, but if it's something you think I should know, I would like you to tell me. I'd rather be hurt by the truth than fooled by a lie."

Veth. It was such a simple request, but it meant they needed to tell her about their past sooner than they'd like. So much for giving her time to get to know them first.

"I can do that," Torren said.

"As can I. But is that all you want?" Zanyr pressed her gently.

"That's all. For now, anyway." Right. She needed more time. They'd already agreed to that, and here he was, pushing for more.

"For now," he agreed, and then let his lips curve up into a wicked grin. "Which means this meaningful moment has ended, and we can get back to what we were doing before we wandered down this unexpected detour."

To his delight, Jenna feigned confusion, her finger tapping at her lips. "Remind me what that was? I seem to have forgotten."

Torren pounced, closing the distance between them so fast he doubted Jenna saw him move at all.

She yelped in surprise as Torren swept her into his arms, turned, and deposited her in the middle of her bed.

"Did that jog your memory?" Zanyr asked as he

unclipped the sheath from his belt and placed it and the dagger inside on a nearby dresser.

"Yes, it did. But now there's a different problem. I need to get back up."

"Why?" Torren growled.

"Because I'm still fully clothed. Or do you want me to try to get out of this dress while lying down?"

Zanyr raked his gaze over their *mahaya's* body. The clothing she wore was unadorned, dull, and covered far too much of her body for Zanyr's liking.

"Do you like that dress?" Zanyr asked.

"It's a dress. It's comfortable and suitable for work. Why?"

Zanyr bent over her, claiming a kiss as he gently caught her by the wrists and pinned her hands over her head. "You asked for honesty, so here it is. It doesn't do you justice. Why do you hide your beauty?"

"I'm not hiding—hey!"

Torren whipped out his blade and used it to slice through the fabric. He started at her neckline and didn't stop until he reached the hem of her skirt. The dress fell away, exposing bare skin and red silk.

"Now that, I like," Zanyr said approvingly. "Red is a better color for you, and the fabric looks as soft and inviting as you do."

"You ruined my dress!"

"I did." Torren set the dagger aside, taking care to put it far out of Jenna's reach. Just in case.

"We'll buy you a replacement." Zanyr pointed to Torren. "He's rich."

"So are you," Torren retorted.

"Well, I'm not." She was riled enough to actually glare at them, which only made him smile. If she was comfortable enough to talk back to them while she was mostly naked and pinned to the bed, things were progressing quickly.

"You are now. Everything we have is yours. You are an equal partner in our lives, *mahaya*. In all matters.

"I... wow." She blinked, stunned. "You aren't getting much out of this deal. I get two hot males and all their worldly goods. In exchange you get... me."

"Don't do that again," Zanyr growled down at her.

"What?" she asked.

"Diminish yourself. Make it seem like you have no worth. You are our *mahaya*. You are our *everything*."

10

———

Reality shuddered and spun, leaving her momentarily adrift. "… our everything." The words kept repeating in her head. She clung to them, barely daring to believe they were true, but at the same time, she knew they were.

They valued her. Wanted her. Had offered her everything they had and asked for nothing in return.

This was more than she'd dared to dream of. So why was she lying back, dazed and silent? She needed to say something.

She opened her eyes and saw them both looking at her. Not just looking. They *saw* her. For the first time in her life, she truly felt seen, and it was everything she wanted but had been afraid to say.

"Yes," was all she said. It was the most complete answer she'd ever given, and she meant it with all of her heart.

Torren leaned down to kiss her, the heat of his mouth branding her lips and making her pulse quicken. She raised her head to kiss him back, but Zanyr still had hold of her wrists. She broke the kiss to tip her head and look at him, and he gave her a wicked little smile.

"Do you want me to release you?" he asked.

She opened her mouth to say yes, but he stopped her with a shake of her head. "Don't answer too quickly. Think about it. Shall I let go, or do you want me to pin you to the bed so you can only squirm and beg for release as Torren starts your first lesson?"

"F-first lesson?" she stammered.

"Mm-hmm," Torren almost purred as he cupped one of her breasts in his hand. "You've never been with two males at once. You have no idea the pleasure we can bring you. It's time you learned."

There it was again—a hint of darkness in his tone. It made her insides quiver when he talked that way. Zanyr had it too, the way he'd explained to her what her choices were. To be free, or to trust them with her body. With her pleasure.

She knew what she wanted. Hell, she'd wanted this from the moment she'd first seen Torren fall from the sky. But thinking it was one thing. Saying it was harder. "I... I want..." She pushed the words past her lips. "I want you to pin me to the bed."

"As you wish," Zanyr whispered the words against her lips before kissing her. His beard rasped against her skin, creating an erotic friction that amplified the need already coursing through her body.

Lost in the kiss she shared with one of her mates, she forgot about Torren until his mouth closed over her nipple, drawing it into the heated depths of his mouth.

She uttered a moan and arched her back, offering herself to them. They accepted her invitation with a hunger that took her breath away. Zanyr's tongue tangled with hers as he pressed her down into the mattress, his mouth slanting across hers while his strong hands held hers over her head.

Torren suckled and teased at her nipples, his fingers, and mouth working in concert. She moaned again, desire building until she couldn't think of anything but the pleasure of their touch.

They were relentless, passionate, and utterly focused on her. Stars above and below. She'd never experienced anything like this with her other lovers.

Torren raised his head, depriving her of his mouth. "Hold her for a second. I need to undress."

Zanyr barely acknowledged his *anrik*'s words, but when Torren rolled away from her, Zanyr took his place. The hard bar of his cock pressed against her thigh as he wrapped himself around her, his mouth and hands laying claim to her body.

"Greedy bastard." Torren laughed from somewhere nearby.

Jenna opened her eyes and got an eyeful of virile, naked Vardarian. Torren's golden scales gleamed as the light played over him, revealing a body as sinful as his smile.

"Wow." Her brain was on autopilot, and what should have been an inside voice moment was instead said out loud.

"Now you've done it," Zanyr chided her with a chuckle. "His ego didn't need a boost."

A well-timed kiss stopped her before she could respond, and by the time it ended, Torren had returned. The bed dipped beneath his weight as he settled himself to one side.

"My turn," Zanyr said, stealing one last kiss before he rolled away.

She kept her eyes on him as he stood and then stripped. His arms and upper torso were thick with muscle and highlighted by the red-gold cast of his scales. His lower body was built just as powerfully, but his scales were bright gold.

"Do I get a wow?" he asked, flexing for her benefit.

Torren ignored the display as he busied himself with guiding her out of the remains of her ruined outfit.

"Wow. Definitely."

Zanyr bowed to her. "Thank you."

"And he says I have an ego." Torren stroked a hand down her stomach, not stopping until his palm covered her mound and his long fingers rested along the seam of her pussy. "Are you ready for your first lesson?"

"Yes. Oh, yes."

Zanyr walked back to the bed, looking thoughtful, and then glanced at Torren.

He must have said something via their link because Torren's eyes brightened and he gave a brisk nod.

"What are you planning?" she asked.

"You'll see," Zanyr said. He stretched out on the opposite side from Torren and then tapped his chest. "Roll over so you're facing Tor."

She complied without thinking about it, earning her a pleased smile from Torren.

A warm hand moved from her shoulder, down her arm, along her flank, and down past her hip. "Leg up," Zanyr coaxed.

He guided her leg upward and back so she was draped over his thigh.

She should have felt exposed like this, her naked body on display, but she didn't. When Torren rolled to face her, she thrilled at the sensation of being caught between their bodies.

Zanyr swept her hair back from the side of her neck and nuzzled the soft patch of skin below her ear. "I've wanted to do this since I first caught your scent on the wind."

Someone, she thought it was Torren, slid a finger into the slick folds of her sex. He stroked her slowly with light teasing touches that only fanned the flames of her desire. She rocked against the pressure of Torren's hand, the gentle motion making Zanyr groan as her ass rubbed over his cock.

Hot, open-mouthed kisses fell on her neck and shoulder while Torren dipped his head to suck on her nipples again. Both of them were pressed against her, hard bodies and harder cocks creating an erotic friction she couldn't get enough of. This had to be the effects of the *sharhal*. It couldn't be like this every time. Could it? She tried to remember what they'd discussed in classes that, at the time, had seemed graphically in-depth. Now she realized they weren't detailed enough.

She let her hands wander, exploring the ridges and planes of her lovers' bodies. She recalled something from one of the classes and slid her hand over Torren's ribs to his back. His wings were folded neatly against his body, and she ran her fingertips along the edge.

Torren shuddered and growled against her skin.

"Do that again," Zanyr encouraged her.

She did, this time working her fingers closer to his spine and the spot between his wings. The result was explosive. Torren groaned and bucked, his cock as hard as hull plating as he ground himself against any part of her he could reach. She used her free hand to grasp his cock, wrapping her fingers around the thick length.

"Qarf!" Torren swore.

"I think our *mahaya* has some lessons of her own to teach," Zanyr said.

"You have... no idea." Torren gasped. He raised his head and met her gaze. "If you do that again, blossom, I will skip the introductory course and move on to something more advanced."

She wanted to learn anything they'd teach her. "Show me everything."

"Witnessed," both of them said in the same breath.

Torren stared at Jenna, enthralled by what he saw. She was so beautiful like this with her body and her heart open and vulnerable. Her trust in them was as powerful an aphrodisiac as the mating fever that burned in his blood.

He watched his *anrik* and their mate for a moment, enjoying the intimacy that could only come from sharing this way. Zanyr held her thigh over the top of his, his other arm beneath her as his hand worked the nub of her nipple. A dot of blood marked a spot on her neck where his fangs had nicked her. They'd have to be careful about that. Neither of them had ever reached these levels of arousal before where their fangs dropped in anticipation of what must happen soon—the bite that would bring their *mahaya* more pleasure than she'd ever known while marking her as their mate forever.

Jenna ran her fingertips over his back again, pushing his control to its breaking point. Who had told her about that spot? Someone must have. If it had been another male... but no. There'd been no scent of anyone else in her home or on her clothes. She hadn't been with anyone else.

She was theirs. And theirs alone.

He flicked his fingers over the swollen bud of her clitoris, smiling at the way she gasped and writhed in response. He already had a sense of what she liked, and he used that information to push her toward orgasm—the first of many she'd experience tonight.

Every breath he took was heavy with the scent of sex and need, the sounds of their pleasure filling the room. She moaned again, and his fangs dropped, his instincts screaming at him to claim her with cock and fangs, letting their bodies merge and their blood mingle.

Soon, but not yet. When they claimed her, it would be in the bed she'd share with them for the rest of their lives in the home they'd made for themselves, far from judgment and the darkness of the past.

Jenna's moans and cries grew louder as he toyed with her clit, working her closer to the edge until she trembled and gasped, almost begging for release. He gave her what she needed before it went that far. She needed to know what she was begging for first.

His eyes met Zanyr's as he pushed her over the brink and into an orgasm. The two of them shared a moment of satisfaction as their female came with a cry that reverberated down to his soul.

They gave her no time to regain her senses as Torren shifted onto his knees and moved to a spot beside her head. Then he took one of her hands and returned it to his cock, which rose, hard and hot, from between his thighs.

When she opened her eyes, he deliberately held up the hand he'd used to pleasure her, making sure she saw when he licked her essence from his fingers.

She opened her mouth to say something, but the only noise she made was a drawn-out moan as Zanyr adjusted himself so that his cock stroked over the folds of her pussy.

"Do you want him to fuck you?" Torren asked.

"Y-yes."

"And what about me?" he drawled, his hand still covering hers as she stroked his cock.

"You want me to make you come? Don't you?"

"Oh, yes. But you can choose how."

While they talked, Zanyr continued to tease her. He rubbed himself over areas already hypersensitive after her previous orgasm.

"Jenna," he called to her, bringing her attention back to him. "Choose. Hands or mouth."

Her fingers tightened around his shaft as she coaxed

him closer. "Mouth." She uttered the word barely a beat before dropping her head and opening her lips to take him inside.

He hissed in surprise and pleasure, his hands tangling in her hair as she plied his length with a surprisingly talented tongue.

"Now that's a sexy sight," Zanyr murmured, watching from his vantage point behind Jenna.

"This is not a reconnaissance mission. Don't you have something you're supposed to be doing right now?" Torren said.

"Right. Right. On it." Zanyr grinned. "Or in this case, in."

Torren felt rather than saw the moment his partner slid himself into her channel. Jenna tensed, and her next moan rolled over her tongue, along his cock, and vibrated his balls. *Fraxx*, that felt good.

They moved together, the push and pull of sex building into a crescendo of pleasure that threatened his control. They chased each other to new heights of pleasure, reveling in their mate's responsiveness. No longer shy or uncertain, she basked in their attention, drinking it in like a goddess accepting the worship she was due.

It didn't take long for the rhythm to falter as all three of them began the final ascent to release. His control slipped and then shattered as she took him deeper, burying him in soft, wet heat.

Zanyr uttered a strangled groan, his thrusts coming faster now.

Torren lifted a hand from her hair to cup one

bouncing breast, his fingers tweaking the diamond hard nub of her nipple until she moaned.

They rode separate waves of pleasure that brought them all to the same place at nearly the same moment.

"Utter perfection," Zanyr said, his voice more growl than words.

Jenna hummed, the sound buzzing over his cock. Something uncoiled deep inside him, and he touched her shoulder in warning.

She only sucked on him harder, and his world shattered around him as she took him over the edge and beyond.

Jenna came so hard Torren felt her body quake with the force of it, her hands shaking as they stroked his cock for every drop of his cum.

Zanyr only lasted a few seconds longer before joining them in a moment of pure ecstasy.

Torren slumped over Jenna, showering her face and hair with kisses while Zanyr pressed his brow to her bare back and fought to catch his breath.

Jenna eventually broke the silence. She raised her head and let his cock slip from between her lips. "Why didn't anyone tell me it would taste this good? It's like candy!"

Torren laughed, his heart overflowing with an emotion he barely recognized—joy. "You taste good too, blossom. So good. I think we'll be feasting on you all night long."

She shivered and sagged back onto the bed. "If you insist."

11

Sʜᴇ ᴛᴏᴏᴋ it as a good sign when her lovers—no, her mates—let her sleep in. One of them was still in bed with her, his big body curled around hers and one arm draped over her waist.

When she forced herself to open her eyes, she discovered her bedmate was Zanyr. A quick sweep with her hand indicated that the other side of the bed was cool. Torren had been up for some time.

Deep, sonorous breathing told her that Zanyr was still asleep, which meant she had a short window of time to check for messages from Shadow.

She eased herself out of bed, careful not to disturb Zanyr. Once she was on her feet, she crept across the room to the closet. She touched the panel and held her breath as the door slid open with a soft whir. Would it be enough to wake him up? She watched for any sign, but Zanyr just rolled onto his side and slept on.

She took the comm from its hiding place and carried it to the one place in the house she wouldn't be disturbed.

The message was brief and had been sent hours ago.

Meet today. Location Charlie-Two. Usual time. And congratulations!

The usual time meant she'd have to find an excuse to be out of the house in about two hours. The location was a simple code she'd committed to memory. Shadow would wait for her inside one of the outbuildings in the part of the colony where the human females stayed while they acclimatized to their new home.

It took just a few seconds to send back a confirmation. That done, she got on with her morning ritual, including a long, luxuriously hot shower. She needed it after last night. Zanyr and Torren were true to their word and had kept her awake until the wee hours of the morning. Last night, she felt as if she could have carried on with them forever, but this morning her thoughts were sluggish, and her body twinged and ached in some interesting places.

The nanotech both males carried offered some benefits she hadn't appreciated until now. Not only were they incredibly fit, but their endurance... *veth.*

She hummed happily to herself as she finished her libations and slipped into a bathrobe she'd bought for herself the first time she'd gone shopping. It was thick, plush, and a deep crimson color she hadn't been able to resist.

Unsure if Zanyr would still be asleep, she hid the comm under a stack of folded towels in a cabinet. She'd put it back in its proper place once she was alone.

It was a good thing she did because Zanyr was sitting up in bed when she entered the room.

"Good morning, *mahaya*." He stretched out his arms and rolled his shoulders. "Did you sleep well?"

"I could use another few hours to recover fully, but yes, I slept wonderfully well."

"Once we claim you, the nanotech will take care of such things. Honestly, I don't know how humans accomplish as much as you do without any enhancements."

"We have coffee for that. And *ja'kreesh* for the days that coffee isn't enough."

"Coffee is good. Torren and I have added that to our morning meal."

That was interesting. "I thought you didn't need stimulants."

Zanyr laughed. "I don't. Vex needs all the help he can get in the mornings. That male does not function well until the sun has been up a few hours."

"It didn't matter what time of day I wanted to wake. The care center had a regimented schedule we all had to comply with. Some of the families I worked for were early risers. Others were later, but I was always expected to be awake and ready to help the children start their day." She shrugged. "I didn't know any other way to be until I came here. Now, I've discovered I am actually a morning person."

"Good. That means you can help me motivate Torren in the mornings. It will be easier with the two of us."

"Wait. If he's not a morning person, why is he up already? And where is he?"

Zanyr grinned smugly. "He's back at the farm.

Someone needed to check on things there. Since he found you, I get to be the one to wake up with you today."

"I hope he found the coffee setting on the dispenser."

"He did." Zanyr tapped a spot behind his ear. "He made sure I heard all about his morning."

"How long has he been gone?"

"An hour or so. He wasn't happy about leaving, but we've got a fair bit to do before we bring you out to the house." He blinked. "*Qarf*. Let me try that again. Jenna, we'd like it if you'd come to our home tonight. We want to show you around and let you see everything."

"I'd like that." The entire class of new colonists had gone to one of the farms surrounding the colony as part of their instruction. Jenna had been stunned by the vast stretches of plants being cultivated. She was curious to see if her mates' farm was the same. Only, the farm wasn't just her mates' home. It would be hers, too.

"We have so much to show you. We designed our place ourselves. It's larger than most of the townhomes, so if you'd like to claim a room or two for yourself, you'll have plenty to choose from."

"What would I need a room for? Never mind two."

"To put things just the way you like them. Torren collects weapons. He likes to dig into the history of other cultures. He's got the start of a little museum in his rooms. I have an office to run the farm's finances and handle any council business, and another that's just a comfortable place to relax when I want to be alone."

The idea of having a space of her own to do anything she wanted was overwhelming. Part of the support she'd received during her integration period was focused on discovering what crafts and hobbies she might enjoy. She'd never had spare time to indulge in such things before, and she hadn't found anything that called to her. Not yet, anyway. But maybe she could use the space to discover what she enjoyed doing.

"I have no idea what I'll do with it, but I think I'd like to have a room like that."

"Then we'll let you pick one for yourself." He rolled out of bed and stretched again, this time extending his wings. "If you like, you can stay with us for a few days. That would give us time to get to know each other. You can always come back here if you need some time alone."

"That sounds good." Her words surprised her. Was she actually ready to do this? She hadn't even talked to Shadow yet, though she couldn't believe her mates were anything but what they appeared to be—good males who, for some inexplicable reason, wanted her. Still, she felt like she was missing something.

It took her several heartbeats to realize what it was. She had no doubts. No voices whispering to her that she wasn't good enough for them. That she didn't deserve happiness.

"What has you smiling like that?" Zanyr asked.

She laughed, and it was more than just a sound. The feeling bubbled up inside her and filled her with light. "I think you and Vex are good for me."

He was in front of her in an instant, his hand on her cheek. "We are. We must be because the ancestors made you for us, which means they also created us for you."

She reached up to cover his hand with hers, rising on her toes to kiss him.

He bowed his head to meet her, his free arm curving around her waist and drawing her in close.

"I think we got out of bed too soon, *ana-thi*." His lips brushed hers in a soft, questing kiss that fanned the flames of a fire she thought had to be quenched by now but weren't.

As the *sharhal* flared to life again, she reached between them and untied the knot in her robe. "I think we did, too."

By the time Zanyr left to help Torren at the farm, Jenna had almost run out of time. She left her overnight bag half packed on the bed. She'd have to finish later. If she didn't leave soon, she'd be late for her meeting. Once she'd spoken to Shadow, she'd be able to tell her *mahoyen* the truth. They wouldn't like it. She already knew that. They wanted to protect her. Discovering she was taking risks to help the colony wasn't going to make them happy. But she'd feel safer continuing her work now that they were in her life.

Zanyr didn't even know yet, and he was already reluctant to leave her alone. When she'd told him she'd be running errands this afternoon, he'd offered to go with her. Any other time, she'd have welcomed his company, but not today. The simple lie she told about her plans ballooned into something bigger as she made excuses as to why she'd rather go on her own.

She wasn't good at lying. She'd never done it before she'd agreed to help Haven this way. Thankfully, Zanyr accepted her reasons and didn't push. She'd have to apologize to him later. Last night, she'd asked them to be honest with her. It didn't sit right that she was still lying to them.

That wouldn't last long, though. Once this meeting was done and she had clearance, she'd tell them everything. If they were as kind and understanding as she believed them to be, they'd forgive her.

12

———

Zanyr flew in ever-ascending circles over Jenna's house but didn't leave the area. Something wasn't right with their *mahaya*, and he wasn't sure what to do about it.

He'd sensed it the moment she left the bed, and he rolled over so he could watch his mate go about her day. The fact she was naked was simply a side benefit.

Jenna's behavior had been odd. She may have tried to be quiet so as not to wake him, but he felt it was more than that. She seemed to be sneaking around her room, even going into her closet to retrieve something that looked like a comm unit. Only her comm was on the dresser. When she'd returned, she didn't have the item with her.

By itself, that incident hadn't been more than a point of interest—something to address at a later time or if it happened again. Then she'd lied to him about what she planned to do today. She'd asked them for honesty, and this was how she behaved? It made no sense. Was she meeting a lover to tell them it was over? That didn't feel like the right answer, but what else could it be? Unless she was another spy recruited by the Shadow Men.

No. She couldn't be. Jenna was no more capable of betraying the colony than of sprouting wings and taking flight. Still considering everything, he decided it was time to let Torren know their mate was up to something.

He gave his *anrik* the details over their link, keeping everything as clinical and brief as he could.

"We need to follow her and find out what she's doing. If she's endangering herself, we'll put a stop to it," Torren replied after several seconds of increasingly creative cursing.

"And if she's a danger to the colony?"

"I don't believe she is. But if I'm wrong, we've got a problem. Do we turn in our mate? What would that do to us? We haven't completed the claiming. If they imprison her somewhere off-world, do we go with her or risk staying here?"

"She's our mate. We go where she goes." This wasn't up for debate as far as he was concerned.

"So where is she right now?" Torren asked.

"Still at home. I'm watching the house. No one in or out." He hated how easy it was to fall back into the old ways. It felt too much like one of their missions. Observing, reporting, and then taking action.

"I'll be there shortly. Keep me updated."

Five minutes later, she left the house. Once again, she was dressed in muted colors with a cream-colored top and dark pants—simple, unadorned, and unremarkable. Now he wondered if her choices were due to personal preference or because she was deliberately trying to avoid notice.

He let Torren know she was on the move.

She didn't move far. Only a few meters from her house, she met up with a Vardarian male. They were too far away to make out details, but he thought the male looked familiar. Maybe someone he'd seen at the tavern? No. The palace? Maybe. He couldn't be sure.

Did Jenna know him? Was this who she was meeting? He got his answer quickly. After a few words of greeting, the male nodded, picked something from one of the fruit trees nearby and offered it to Jenna.

She took it, waved, and went on her way. Just an interaction between neighbors. Nothing of import. He continued to follow her, careful to stay high enough she wouldn't be able to spot him.

After a few minutes, he had a good idea where she was headed, and once she crossed the bridge, he was certain. He let Torren know where to meet him and made his descent. The tree cover would make it impossible to follow her from the air, so they'd go overland from here.

Why the *fraxx* was Jenna headed back to the human camp? No one was there now. The place would be empty until the next batch of colonists arrived. Nothing about this felt good.

They'd follow her and find out what she was doing. Then, the three of them would have a long talk about honesty, trust, and other fun topics.

Jenna munched on the fruit Sanjin had given her. She didn't know its name, but she would have to find out. It was delicious. Tart and crisp, it reminded her a little of an apple, only it was a mottled green and more square than round.

She enjoyed the opportunity to wander through Haven, even if today's walk had an important purpose.

As she walked, she let her mind wander. She was glad that at least one of her neighbors was friendly. Tani would probably be thrilled that Jenna was moving out to live with Torren and Zanyr. Or not, given the female's reaction to seeing her with them.

Sanjin had welcomed her the first day she moved in. He'd gifted her with a basket of fruits and vegetables from his own garden and pointed out the nearest shops and restaurants. She'd often run into him during her morning walks, and they always exchanged greetings. His *anrik* worked on the orbital platform, and Sanjin kept hinting he'd like to invite her over for dinner the next time he returned to the planet. She got the feeling that dinner was code for a lot more than just a meal, so she'd politely declined. Now she was glad she had. This situation was strange enough without involving anyone else in her sudden change in marital status.

Oddly, she hadn't flushed or felt awkward when she'd spoken to Sanjin today. He was attractive enough that she'd always felt flustered around him before. Was this another aspect of the *sharhal*? Maybe. She knew the bonding process ensured that no Vardarian ever desired anyone besides their mates. So far, all the human females involved with the other species had reacted the same way.

It didn't take her long to weave through the shoppers on the bridge. A few vehicles eased their way through the crowd, but all of them were headed into town, not out toward the camp.

Haven had expanded since the first arrivals, and now a number of homes and businesses populated what the locals still called the far side of the river. No one noticed as she made her way past the various buildings. Her feet marched to the steady beat of a hammer that rang out from the yard behind a shop that specialized in weapons. Anya's mates owned and ran the place, which was why it was so close to the tavern. Her daily commute only took a few minutes.

Thoughts of commutes and how she'd get from the farm to the education center occupied her mind for the remainder of the trip. She approached the designated building and knocked sharply in a four-beat pattern.

The door opened immediately.

"Come on in." Shadow gestured her inside.

The interior was dim, and the air smelled faintly of dust, despite the fact the place had only been empty for a short time.

"Hello, Jenna," another voice greeted her. Female. Friendly.

Shadow pointed into a distant corner, where she spotted another figure. "This is Skye. I've been acting as a go-between for the two of you since it would be a bit obvious if you were to start having regular meetings with a member of the prince's security staff.

Skye. She put the name and face together quickly. "You're mated to Yardan. The prince's spymaster."

"I am." The woman moved out of the shadows. Both women were cyborgs, with more strength and power than Jenna could imagine. "And speaking of mates, congratulations to you! I actually bet Shadow a dinner out that you would show up with at least one of your new mates in tow. How did you convince them to let you come alone?"

"Please, share your secret. I've had to threaten mine with bodily harm on occasion. It turns out that Torskis are almost as possessive and overprotective as Vardarians."

"They're busy getting things ready at the farm. They want me to stay with them for a few days, and Zan said they'd need time to get ready." She cocked her head. "And they don't know I'm here. I haven't told them anything. I didn't think it was safe to do that until I'd spoken to Shadow."

"You didn't tell them?" Shadow smacked her forehead lightly. "Of course you didn't because we made it clear that you couldn't tell anyone. I'm sorry, Jenna. That couldn't have been an easy choice."

"It wasn't. So, does this mean I can tell them? There's no reason not to? I mean, they're not a risk or anything?"

"Zan and Torren are good males," Shadow reassured her. "And they are lucky to have found a mate as wonderful as you are."

"I did a background check on both of them as soon as I heard," Skye said. "You can tell them. They'll get incredibly protective. Which is good. You'll be safer with them than anywhere outside the palace walls. Those two are some of the most dangerous males in the colony."

Jenna scowled. "But we'll be outside the main colony. How is that safer? I mean, they are obviously warriors, big, scary ones. But Zan is just a farmer and Torren is a teacher. How dangerous can they be?"

Skye looked at Shadow, who had a confused expression on her face, too. "Oh *fraxx*. You don't know.

"Know what?" Jenna demanded.

Skye held up a finger as her gaze when distant.

"Incoming message," Shadow explained and tapped her temple.

After what felt like forever, Shadow sighed and dropped her hand. "You can ask them yourself. They followed you here."

Jenna was stunned. She'd been followed? She hadn't noticed. And why had they done that?

Because she'd lied to them. That's why. The answer was so obvious she winced a little.

Shadow came over and patted her shoulder in sympathy. "You did nothing wrong. Stand tall and don't take any crap from them. If they're anything like mine, they're bound to say or do something annoying. Just remember, they might act like idiots. But they are *your* idiots."

"And everything they do is because they care about you," Skye added. "Repeat as many times as needed. Oh, and welcome to the club. We meet on Tuesdays."

"We should be ashamed of ourselves," Zanyr muttered out of the side of his mouth.

"We? What's this *we* crap. I wasn't the one who gave away our position by sneezing at the worst possible moment," Torren shot back.

"You're the one who stirred up the dust when you landed. I've seen younglings on their first flight make better landings."

One of their captors coughed. "Actually, we just followed the sound of bickering, and there you were."

"Shut up, Edge," Zanyr snapped.

"You want to go for round two? I'm ready if you are." The dark-haired de facto leader of the cyborgs turned back to them, one fist raised. He was sporting a split lip, and his clothes were covered in dust and detritus from the forest ground.

"That depends. Are you going to throw a decent punch this time?" Zanyr smirked at Edge. The cyborg sat on the council with him, and while they weren't exactly friends, he had a deep respect for the male.

"Stop goading him," Kade interrupted them. "In fact, everyone, stop goading everyone. You're giving me a headache."

Edge rolled his eyes at the Vardarian walking beside him. "Stop being dramatic."

They all walked in silence for several seconds.

"So, can I ask where we're headed?" Zanyr asked as he tried to remove some of the dust and debris from the vest Torren had brought for him.

"You wanted to know what your *mahaya* was up to. You'll get the chance to ask her yourself."

Fraxx. "She knows we're here?" he asked.

"If she doesn't know yet, she will soon. She was attending a very important meeting. Or did you think we were out here guarding an empty camp for the fun of it?" Kade said.

"We didn't know you were here at all," Zanyr retorted. The admission cost him some pride, but it was the truth. They were out of practice.

"Who are you guarding? And why is Jenna involved?" Torren asked, his voice sharp.

Kade lifted one wing in a shrug. "I'm guarding my mate. Edge is with me because I asked him to come. The rest, you'll have learn from someone else because I have no idea."

"You don't know why your mate is out here having a secret meeting?" Zanyr stared at Kade. "Why not?"

Kade grinned back. "Because I've been mated long enough to learn a few things." He ticked off the points on his fingers. "Fact one, if I don't know, I can't get in trouble for repeating something to the wrong being at the wrong time. Fact two, my mate is a badass cyborg assassin who is quite capable of tearing my wings off if I annoy her too much. Fact three, I trust her. If I needed to know, she'd tell me."

Edge snickered. "This is one of the many reasons I'm glad I'm not mated. This relationship crap is complicated."

All three of them turned to look at Edge. "What?"

"Denial is not a good look for you," Kade said.

"I'm not denying anything. I'm. Not. Mated."

"I never said you were," Zanyr said.

"We just don't believe you're glad about it," Torren finished.

Edge flipped them off with both hands. "All of you can shut up now."

When the door opened, Jenna half expected her mates to storm in and start demanding answers. Instead, they were shoved through the doorway by two males—one cyborg and one Vardarian. All four of them were dirty, disheveled, and had a collection of scrapes, cuts, and bruises.

"Kade. What happened?" Shadow demanded before Jenna could.

"We caught these two sneaking around. They uh, resisted," Kade said.

"Resisted what? They're not strangers for *fraxx* sake. You know who they are."

Jenna stifled a giggle. So this was Shadow's mate.

Kade shrugged. "We got a little carried away."

Shadow threw up her hands. "Next time, I'm asking Denz to provide security. I told you it was just a precaution, and there was next to no chance of any trouble."

"When have you known any of us to walk away from a chance to spar?" the cyborg asked.

"Since never, which is why I was happy not to be mated to a cyborg. But now I see you're corrupting him."

Kade snorted. "I was corrupt before we even met. It's one of the things you love about me."

Jenna finally had enough and did something unusual. She raised her voice. "Excuse me. Hello? My turn to talk." She turned to look at her mates. "What are you doing here?"

Zanyr and Torren looked at each other and then at her. "You checked for messages on a secret comm unit and then lied about what you'd be doing this afternoon. We wanted to know why."

She groaned and buried her face in her hands. This had all gone wrong. "Fair enough," she spoke without removing her hands. "But then we need to have a conversation about who you are, and why Skye thinks you're two of the most dangerous males in the colony."

13

Torren quieted his mind and tried to focus as Jenna explained. From time to time, Shadow or Skye chimed in to clarify something or to give more context.

"You're a spy?" Torren asked at the end. He'd heard it, but he still couldn't believe it.

"Technically, she's a double agent," Edge pointed out. "And I'm not happy to find out we're running these kinds of ops without the leadership council being read in to the situation."

"The council didn't need to know. Now, all of you are going to be sworn to secrecy. Yardan is going to shed his scales when he finds out about this breach. You all know my *mahoyen*, and none of you want to get on his bad side." Skye arched one brow. "Right?"

Everyone nodded.

"Edge is right. I am a double agent. I'm also not very good at it. The first time I needed to do something stealthy and spy-like, this happened." Jenna threw out her hands to encompass the knot of people gathered. "I think I should retire."

"Yes," Zanyr and Torren said in one breath.

"Maybe," Skye said.

"What?" Torren's half-rose from his chair. "She can't continue." He realized he was almost shouting and lowered his voice. "Sorry, Jenna. I'm not trying to make this decision for you, but I'm glad you see things clearly. This is too dangerous." He glowered at Skye. "And I cannot believe anyone asked you to do it in the first place!"

"She came to us," Skye shot back. "The enemy recruited her first. Jenna had the courage to risk everything, including her chance to come here, to tell us. That took a measure of bravery I'm not sure many of us could match."

Kade looked at Jenna with admiration. Torren fought back the urge to growl at the other male.

Skye ignored everyone and continued talking. "As for her effectiveness? Jenna is the reason we found the other spy in her class so quickly." The cyborg turned to Jenna, her expression fierce. "Do not sell yourself short. The work you've done has been invaluable. You *are* good at this. Whatever you decide, you need to remember that. You helped protect Haven in a way no one else could have."

"Thank you, Skye, but it isn't that big a deal. I was only doing what I thought was right."

"And bravery." Zanyr reached out and took Jenna's hand. She sat between them with the others grouped around in a rough circle. "I know how hard it can be to do the right thing."

Torren took her other hand. "And how tempting it is to make the easy choice."

Jenna nodded and then stiffened a little. "Was that why you didn't tell me the truth about who you are? Because it was the easy way out?"

Torren wanted to tell her this wasn't the time or place to talk about it. He didn't want to share his past with everyone in this room. Right now, the only one with that information was Skye, and judging by the guilty looks she kept sending their way, she hadn't meant to betray any secrets. That didn't do much to fix the situation, but at least she hadn't done it out of malice.

As much as he didn't want to have this discussion here or now, he also knew they had to. Their actions today had forced Jenna to reveal her secret, and that had put her at risk. The more beings who knew, the higher the chance someone would slip up and put her in danger.

He looked at Zanyr, who nodded, grim faced. "Everything we told you was the truth, Jenna. I'm a chemistry teacher, like one of my fathers. My family still live on Vardaria Prime and are active members of the royal court."

Zanyr picked up the thread of the conversation. "I am an agriculturalist. So is most of my family. What we didn't tell you was that both of us left home not long after reaching adulthood. We were young, stubborn, and certain we wanted to do more with our lives than our family envisioned."

"So you ran away from home?"

"I didn't run," Torren stated. "But I did walk away

after a particularly nasty fight with two of my parents. My second father, the chemistry teacher, told me that if I wanted something else out of life, I'd have to find it on my own. He was right. I packed my things and left that night. He gave me enough money to get off the planet and made me promise to keep in touch."

Kade whistled. "I never put it together. Vex, as in Aristol Vex? *That* family?"

"That family," Torren confirmed.

"So when they..." Kade broke off.

"I'd been gone for years by then. I sent back what I could. It was enough to keep them aloft until a fair wind blew in a change of fortune."

Jenna coughed. "That's fascinating, and I'm going to want to hear all the details about your family later, but for now, will one of you please answer my question? Why are you so dangerous?"

Zanyr sighed. "We hadn't met yet, but we were both on similar paths. We quickly discovered that life on our own wasn't easy. Everything in the galaxy cost money. Neither of us had much of it and no way to earn more. There came a moment when I had to decide if I was going to go home or do something different."

"You did something different," Jenna breathed.

"I did. And that's how we wound up being recruited to Starfall. We signed up within a month of each other."

Kade leaned back in his chair. "Holy *fraxx*."

"I don't understand. What's this Starfall?" Jenna asked.

"A crew of mercenaries with a legendary reputation,"

Kade said. "One of the few mercenary bands run by and for Vardarian warriors."

Jenna still didn't understand. "So, you were soldiers of fortune. What's so wrong about that?"

Torren answered with the pure and simple truth. "Fighting for honor, for glory, or for the defense of the empire are acceptable. Fighting for money is not. When we joined Starfall, we lost our citizenship and the right to go home."

Zanyr nodded. "We were with Starfall for almost two decades. In the end, we couldn't stomach the fighting anymore. It never stopped. Every week we had a new assignment, and some of them were..." He broke off. "You don't need to hear about that right now."

"I'm sorry. I can't imagine what that would be like. But you left. And now you're here. Why is all of this a secret?"

Torren took up the tale again. "Because we aren't citizens of the empire anymore. We didn't have the right to even apply for a place in the diaspora. I went to my family and begged them to intercede on our behalf. My father refused. My second father convinced my mother to help. They went to see Prince Tyran and told him about us. He offered us a place in the colony.

He turned to smile at Skye. "A decision your *mahoyen* did not agree with. He interviewed us more than a dozen times on the voyage here. We convinced him that we were truly looking to leave that life behind us."

"I can only imagine. And on behalf of the cranky son

of a starbeast that he used to be, I apologize for what he must have put you through."

Everyone laughed at that, and some of the tension left the room.

"So you're not supposed to be here? Is that why this is a secret?"

"The empress would not be happy if she knew her brother had allowed exiles to join his colony. But the real reason is this: Not everyone here would accept us if they knew. Old ways die hard, even here. The prince and the spymaster both agreed it would be best not to tell anyone."

Edge snorted. "Please. They want to keep your past a secret because they're worried some of the colonists will be afraid of you. I hate to point this out, but you have several hundred cyborgs running around the colony already, and we're so dangerous the humans wanted to destroy us in our cryo-chambers. So you were mercenaries. Big deal. If the colonists can accept us, they'll accept the two of you. Hell, you're even the same species."

Everyone stared at the cyborg in shock. "What?" Edge demanded. "It's obvious."

Jenna let go of his and Zanyr's hands, popped out of her chair, and ran over to hug Edge. "You're right! And you said it so well. Thank you."

Edge froze, his hands stiff at his sides. "What are you doing?"

"Hugging you."

"Stop it. Humans aren't supposed to hug cyborgs. At least, not this one."

"Why not?" Jenna asked.

Kade stood between Torren and Edge, his hands locked on Torren's shoulders to keep him in the chair while Shadow held down Zanyr.

"For starters," Kade drawled, "you should remember that your mates are still in the thrall of the mating fever. Touching other males is *not* a good idea."

"Oops." Jenna let go of Edge and hurried back to Torren. "I'm sorry. I didn't realize. I just… Edge was right. I was so happy that all our secrets are out in the open now." She laid a hand on his cheek, and he immediately began to calm down.

"I'm yours. I always will be. You and Zan are my family now."

"Damn right we are." Zanyr glared at Edge for another moment and then exhaled. He looked at the cyborg still gripping his shoulders. "Thanks for the help, Shadow. I lost my head for a second there."

"No problem." The cyborg female walked over to Kade and the two retreated back to their chairs.

To Torren's relief, the meeting broke up not long after. They all agreed not to talk about anything they'd learned today, though Zanyr and Edge were already having a side conversation about how long until the rest of the council was informed.

Jenna didn't leave her chair. She sat quietly, her small hand wrapped around several of his fingers. They wouldn't have long before the *sharhal* flared again, but for the moment, they were all thinking clearly. That was a good thing because they had some more talking to do.

"You ready to go?" he asked her.

"Yes." She turned her head his way. "But I think we should walk back. Together."

"I agree." It would give them the time they needed.

Zan returned as they rose from their seats. He nuzzled Jenna's cheek for several seconds in silence and then straightened up. "Home?"

"Home," Torren agreed.

"Which one?" Jenna asked.

"Yours first. Then ours. If that's still okay with you?" Zanyr asked.

She actually sighed with relief. "So the plan hasn't changed?"

"Not unless you want it to," Torren said. He wanted to make it clear that she could change her mind at any time.

"There's no reason to change anything. We're still mated. And I am looking forward to seeing your home."

Zanyr kissed the crown of her hair. "It's *our* home now."

14

———

IT WAS surprising how quickly the others vanished. Kade picked up Shadow and launched himself into the air. Skye and Edge went in separate directions, sprinting away so fast Jenna's eyes only saw blurs of movement that were gone before she could blink.

"Well, that was fun. Let's never do it again," Zanyr muttered.

Jenna looked up and gave him a wry smile. "You brought this on yourself. If you'd waited a few hours, I would have told you everything. I only wanted Shadow's confirmation that I could... what did Edge call it? Read you in."

"And we planned on telling you the truth about our past. We thought it wouldn't hurt to give you more time to get to know us before we told you who we used to be," Torren said.

"I get it. We had a lot going on in a very short amount of time." She took a step forward and her mates followed suit. "And before you say anything, I know it wasn't fair of me to ask for honesty when I wasn't telling you everything."

They walked down the tree-lined road that would take them home. Dappled sunlight played across the hard-packed dirt, and a chorus of birdsong and insect noise made a kind of music in the background.

They talked the whole way back. At first, they answered each other's questions about the past and then switched to talk of the future as they neared the bridge and other beings.

Jenna still had a thousand questions, but those could wait. She didn't care about who they'd been because she'd seen who they were now. Her mates. Two males who wanted to live in peace in a place that welcomed them. They had that in common.

"Come in. There's one more thing I want to tell you about."

It felt good to lead them upstairs and show them the comm unit she'd hidden beneath the towels. "This was how I communicated with Shadow. I'll give it back to her once everything is dealt with."

Torren inspected it carefully. "That's military-grade gear. Even the princess would have trouble cracking the encryption cipher this thing uses."

"Then it's a good thing she's on our side," Jenna said.

"What about the other guys? How do you communicate with them?" Zanyr asked with a scowl. "You've never given them a name, but I am assuming they're part of the Shadow Men?"

"I think of them as the enemy. They told me they were a collection of concerned galactic citizens, but I never believed them. I'm certain they're with the Shadow Men, but it's possible they're not. Other groups have a grudge against the colony. Torex, for example."

"True," Torren agreed. "I try not to think too much about how many beings out there want this colony to fail."

"Not long after I arrived here, a package appeared at the door of my habi-pod. My name was printed on the label, along with a three-digit code I'd been given when I agreed to work for the enemy. Inside was a comm unit not much different from this one, and instructions about basic functions, where to hide it, and how often to check in. One of the first rules is that I must always be alone when I go near its hiding place."

"And where is that?" Zanyr asked.

"It's under a rock in my backyard."

"Why outside?" Torren asked.

"Because I have nightmares about getting them mixed up and sending the wrong information to the wrong side." She'd even put a spot of bright pink paint on the one from Shadow to make sure that didn't happen.

Zanyr winced. "Yeah. That is a damned good reason."

"I want to tell them I'm quitting. But I don't want to break any rules when I do. I want to give them every reason to let me walk away." She sighed. "Though I know that isn't likely. They're not going to take this well. Are they?"

"Probably not." Torren set a comforting hand on her shoulder, and she leaned into his touch. The embers of desire flickered to life again, but she did her best to ignore them for now. She had to keep her head clear for a little while longer.

"But you'll be safe with us. We'll protect you, Jenna. Torren will keep an eye on you while you're working, and one of us can go with you until we're certain there won't be any fallout. The colony is alert for trouble these days, and all new arrivals are carefully vetted. Hells, most of visitors have to remain on the platform and can't come to the surface at all." Zanyr's words sounded good, but she heard the concern laced beneath the confident delivery.

"Nothing has changed. Not really. I knew the risks when I agreed to this. I have to admit, I'm glad it's over. I can't stand lying, and I've done far too much of that since this all started." Guilt and regret made her lapse into silence. Then she realized what she was doing. Hiding her feelings never helped. It was time to try something different. "I feel guilty, though. Like I'm being selfish. If I stop this, am I letting everyone down?"

"No." Zanyr shook his head hard. "There is nothing selfish about you. Don't feel guilty for doing what you need to do to protect yourself. That makes you a lot smarter than me and Torren. When we first thought about leaving, we didn't. We stayed for the wrong reasons."

Torren took over, and she quietly marveled at how easily they managed to continue each other's thoughts. "You're leaving for the right reasons. And, yeah, I'll admit I'm biased when it comes to you, but even if you weren't our *mahaya*, I wouldn't blame you for stepping back. I wish we'd made a different choice back then. I have a lot of regrets, but none of them are about leaving. If that's what you want to do, listen to your heart, and do it. You've done enough for everyone else already."

"More than enough," Zanyr agreed.

It was exactly what she needed to hear. Their poignant logic and belief in her drowned out her doubts. "Then that's what I'll do. But for that to happen, I need to be alone."

"Are you asking us to go?" Torren asked.

His question made her heart ache. "Not exactly. You just can't be with me while I do this." She bit her lip. She didn't want them to leave, but she needed to do this alone. If the enemy had some way of knowing she had company... it wouldn't end well. "Why don't you go home and come back in an hour or so?"

"We're not leaving without you." Torren folded his arms across his chest and glared at her. It made him look even bigger, but that's all. She knew he'd never hurt her.

Zanyr was the one who suggested the oblivious compromise. "Why don't we go outside. It's a nice day, and I saw a fruit stand down the road. We can pick up something and come back a little later."

Jenna brightened. "Oh, that's Sanjin's stand. He grows some of the most amazing fruit. He paid to ship saplings here. Can you believe it? It must have cost the moon and stars, but they're already producing fruit."

Zanyr brightened. "Is that so? Interesting. Come on, Vex. Let's go take a look. I never thought about a fruit orchard, but it might be a viable market option."

"Oh fun. We're going to talk farming stuff." Torren turned and pointed at her. "You keep your comm close at all times and tell us if anything happens. We won't be far away."

"Of course I will. But what are the odds of something happening to me in my own house? Shoo, both of you. And if you see Sanjin, be sure to ask about the fruit he gave me earlier. It was amazing, and I have no idea what it's called."

With them out of the house, the place felt weirdly empty. Even though they'd only been there a single night, their absence was a tangible thing. She'd blame the *sharhal* for that. The mating fever was messing with her head.

She looked around the place, waiting for a pang of... something. She'd only just moved in here. It was the first place she'd ever actually owned. She should be sad, or nostalgic. Shouldn't she? Instead, she was glad she hadn't been here long enough to mess the place up. The paint was still perfect. The counters gleamed. It would make someone else a lovely home.

It only took a minute to retrieve the comm from its hiding place out back. She stood in the sunshine, enjoying the way the heat sank into her back even though the wind was chilly. Summer was almost over. In a matter of weeks, she'd get to experience her first snowfall.

She'd done her part for the colony. Now, it was time for her to live for herself.

With that thought in mind, she started typing. First, her three-digit code, followed by what she hoped was a concise message.

This will be my last report. I have no new intel to relay. I am no longer comfortable with our arrangement and feel the risk of discovery is increasing. I forfeit all agreed upon arrangements. I will destroy this device within twenty-four hours.

She'd never written a resignation letter before. This one felt a little flat, but it would have to do.

A touch of a button and the message was sent. How long would it take to be relayed to her mysterious handler? She had no idea, though it would likely be days. That's how long most of their communications were delayed. A few days to get there, a few days for a reply. She hoped they were a long way from here. If the distance was great enough, maybe they'd forget about her.

She went back inside, the comm unit still in her hand. She'd get rid of it tomorrow. Before they had time to send another message.

Partway up the stairs, she had a dizzy spell. Probably dehydration. She hadn't had anything but coffee today, and that was a few hours ago.

By the time she reached the top, her stomach was roiling. Damn it. Was she coming down with something?

"I should have let them bite me last night," she muttered. Nanotech would kill whatever bug she'd contracted. The timing was terrible. She was supposed to be getting ready to see their home and spend a few days getting to know her mates in and out of the bedroom.

Damn, damn, and triple damn. She didn't want to be sick.

It wasn't until her vision went gray that she began to worry, and then, she was on the floor.

15

———

Zanyr sorted through the various fruits and vegetables available at the stand, curious to see what was on offer. Whoever this Sanjin was, he'd managed to grow a number of Vardarian plants in the local soil, and judging by the size of the produce, he'd been very successful at it.

"I need to talk to this male and find out what his secret is. Do you see this?" He held out a *sazra* as big as his palm.

Torren looked and grunted. "Big. I take it that's unusual?"

"You're hopeless. Yes, it's unusual. None of my crops are doing this well. Granted, this is a small plot, so he can give the plants more attention, but still. I'm impressed."

He was also a tad suspicious. Like everything else in Haven, agriculturists had rules they had to follow. No artificial supplements in the soil, no chemicals, or pesticides. The soil had to stay healthy, and nothing could be allowed to contaminate the land or water.

The only ways he knew to grow produce like this all

involved violating the rules. It was more proof that the colony had grown big enough to need more oversight. He'd bring it up at the next meeting.

Torren had a selection of produce set to one side. "Do you think Jenna would like these?"

"I have no idea. They're some of our favorites, though. So we might as well get them and see what she thinks."

"What fruit do you think she was talking about earlier? There are a few here."

Zanyr lifted his wings in a shrug. "Get one of each? It's got to be one of these."

His comm buzzed at that moment, and he fished it out of his pocket. If the council was calling another meeting right now, he'd refuse to attend.

It was an incoming call from Jenna. Audio only. "Hello, *ana-thi*. You miss us already?"

Silence. "Jenna?" he called her name.

He heard a distant sound, a single word spoken in a barely there whisper that made his blood run cold. "Help."

He spun on his heel and ran back toward her house. As he ran, he kept calling her name, but the line stayed quiet. Even running flat out, it felt like an eternity before he reached her front door.

It was locked.

He screamed in frustration as Torren appeared at his side. "What's wrong?"

"Jenna! She asked for help, but now I can't get her to answer. We need to get in there!"

"Window." Torren was already moving toward the

nearest window. He pulled out his dagger and slammed it pommel first into the center of the glass. It shattered under the blow.

They used their bare hands to clear enough space to squeeze through, ignoring the damage the glass did to them as they worked. In seconds they were inside, both of them bleeding from dozens of small wounds. Not that it mattered. They barely noticed their injuries. Nothing mattered but getting to Jenna.

"You take this floor, I'll take upstairs," he sent to Torren.

"Don't get yourself killed. Dead males can't help anyone."

He didn't bother to respond. There was a time for caution and procedure. This was not one of them. He ignored the stairs and launched straight into the air. Torren would clear the ground floor and ensure there were no surprises, but something in his gut told Zanyr that their mate was upstairs.

There. He spotted her sprawled face down on the floor, not far from her bedroom door. He made it to her side in seconds, the downdraft from his approach making her hair blow in wild tangles around her head, but she didn't move.

"Jenna!"

He dropped to his knees beside her, barely resisting the urge to pull her to him. She could be injured. She must be. But where? He raked his gaze over her and the floor. No blood. Good.

He touched the back of one outstretched hand. Her skin was cooler than it should be. He swept back her hair so he could see at least part of her face. Her complexion was grayish, her lips tight in a rictus of pain that made his stomach twist.

Poison? Illness? What was wrong with her?

"*Mahaya.* I'm here. Speak to me if you can."

Her lashes fluttered and one eye cracked open a little, but he saw no awareness in her gaze.

Then she moaned. The low, pained breath leaked out of her lungs in a slow wheeze.

"Thank the ancestors. Jenna. Stay with me. Do not go to sleep. You have to stay awake."

She didn't answer, but her lashes fluttered.

"Torren! Get up here! I found her."

He'd found her, but he had no idea what was wrong or how to fix it. He'd seen enough death to recognize the signs. Jenna was alive, but she wouldn't be for long. Something was killing her.

Torren landed beside him. "What happened?"

"I have no idea." He touched the side of her neck. Her skin was clammy, and her pulse was faint beneath his fingers. "I know how to treat battle injuries but not something like this. She's not bleeding. I don't see any blaster burns."

"Then it's something internal." Torren looked as frustrated as he felt. "I've already sent out an alert. Help is coming."

"It won't be here soon enough." Something dark and terrible tore open Zanyr's heart. "We're losing her."

"No. We can't." Torren sat down and carefully drew her head onto his lap. "We finally got what we'd dreamed of. I will not let her go."

They looked at each other. "There's only one way."

It wasn't the way they'd imagined claiming their beloved *mahaya*, but if this worked, they would have time to make it up to her.

"Who does it?" Torren asked.

Zanyr lifted her hand, cradling the limp flesh in his. "We do it together."

They claimed her, mixing their blood with hers and gifting her with the only thing they knew might save her life.

Torren crouched over Jenna, willing her to live. They both whispered to her, a litany of adoration and encouragement.

"Come back to us," he kept saying.

At first, he didn't think the nanotech transfusion had worked. She lay so still, her breathing shallow and her golden skin a disquieting shade of gray.

"Do you see?" Zanyr asked? "Look at her mouth. She's not in pain anymore."

Torren saw the change, but he didn't know what it meant. Was she getting better, or was this the end? "Blossom, you have to live because I can't do this without you. One day wasn't enough."

Was she getting warmer? Torren wanted to think so, but it was so hard to be sure. Yes, her color was improving. Her fingers moved next, and he took his first deep breath since he'd seen her lying so still.

"She's still with us."

Zanyr swiped at his eyes with the back of one bloody hand. All he managed to do was to smear streaks of red across his face. "Welcome back, *mahaya*."

They stayed with her until help arrived. A veritable army of help. Medics and healers swarmed into the house while members of the royal guard took up positions around the doors and windows.

"You have to move so we can help her," a human female said.

He focused on her face. He knew her. Dr. Clark. "Is she going to be okay?"

"I think so. Whatever happened, the nanotech you gave her seems to have stabilized her. At least for now." She looked him over, and he realized he was still bleeding. "What *did* happen?"

"We don't know. We only left her alone for a few minutes. Then Zanyr got a call. She asked for help and then the line went dead. We broke into the house to get to her."

"Ah. I wondered." The doctor cast a learned eye over his injuries. "Do you need treatment, or do you want to let the nanotech take care of it?"

He kissed Jenna's hand and then placed it carefully on her stomach. "I'll be fine. I have something I need to do. If there are any issues, I'll see to them later. You take care of her for us. Please."

"I will."

Zanyr was already on his feet, and he reached down to help Torren rise. They moved aside, allowing the medical staff more room to work.

"She was holding this." Zanyr showed him a comm

unit. "I think this is the one from outside. She must have sent the message."

It made sense. They couldn't be sure she'd done it until they spoke to her or cracked the encryption. But it was the most likely scenario.

"I don't like it. She told them she was quitting, and immediately afterward this happens? It's not a coincidence."

Torren kept his voice low and casual, as if they weren't discussing the attempted murder of their mate. "I agree with you. But think about the timeline. She couldn't have sent that message more than half an hour ago. How far do you figure it traveled in that time?"

Zanyr bared his fangs. "Not very *fraxxing* far. Whoever read the message is in the system."

"I think they're closer than that. They'd have to be. Because not only did they receive the message, but they were in a position to react immediately, and they needed access to Jenna to pull this off. Whoever they are, they're here. In Haven."

They locked eyes, both of them understanding what had to happen next. Without a word, they touched wrists, scar to scar.

Zanyr lifted the comm unit. "I'll get this to someone who can crack the encryption."

"And I'll order up our party favors."

Zanyr snorted. "You mean the ones you swore we'd never need to use?"

"Shut up. That was then. This is now." He looked back to where Jenna was being loaded onto a stretcher. "This time, we're going to war for the right reasons."

16

Zanyr wasn't surprised to see Skye outside. She stood out of the way, watching everything with hard, unhappy eyes. He trotted over, and she nodded in greeting.

"Is this when you tell me what the *fraxx* happened?"

"Highlights only. Jenna collapsed. She's only alive because we gave her our nanotech, and it was a near thing." He handed her the comm. "She was holding this when we found her. We think she sent her resignation shortly before whatever happened."

He had to watch his words to avoid giving away information to anyone who might be listening, and it was frustrating the hell out of him.

Skye's lips thinned and her eyes went cold as steel. "They couldn't have responded that fast."

"Not unless they have someone local."

"*Fraxx.* That's not good."

"It's not. You may want to ask your *mahoyen* about locking down all departures until we get some answers."

That got her attention. "Who is we? Because the last time I checked, you weren't a member of the palace guard, cyber security, or the rangers. You need to leave it to us."

Zanyr raised his brow. "They tried to kill our mate. If the prince himself told me to stand down, I wouldn't do it."

"Fine. But when this is over, you can bet I'm going to use this as a hammer to knock some sense into the rest of the council. It's more than time we had some proper law enforcement in Haven."

"You'll have my backing."

"Great. Glad to hear it. Go find your answers and try to keep the damage to a minimum." She frowned. "Do you need weapons? I can authorize access to the main armory."

He grinned. "Not needed. We brought our own."

"You're not supposed to have your own weapons. Colony rules! Remember?"

He walked away and called back over his shoulder. "Too bad we don't have anyone to enforce those rules yet."

He tracked down Torren, and the two of them jogged to a relatively empty area not far from the *gharshtu* pens. The noise and stench from the herds of scaly, foul tempered creatures deterred most visitors, which made it perfect for their needs.

The drone had a fully programmed autopilot and enough power to make the trip from the woods where they'd stashed their weapons cache in a matter of minutes.

Torren was against the idea, but Zanyr had convinced him it was better to be prepared. It turned out that smuggling weapons onto the planet was easy. Weapons acquisition was one of the many services Hezza B. was happy to provide once they convinced her it was for the protection of the colony.

Donning the armor and arming up brought back memories Zanyr didn't want to dwell on. This was different. This wasn't about money. They were protecting their family and their home.

"I don't want to get used to this," Torren said. "But I'll admit I missed the armor. Do you think I could talk Director Firt into letting me wear it in class?"

"I doubt it. But if you're scared of a bunch of wet-behind-the-wings students..."

"Yeah. Yeah. No armor in the classroom." Torren slapped a gauntleted hand to his armored chest. "Now, where do we want to start?"

"With Jenna's judgmental neighbor. The female."

"Jenna said her name is Tani."

"Noted." Zanyr slid a second blaster into a holster near his ankle. "Let's pay Tani a visit."

With the street outside Jenna's house still full of curious onlookers and guards, they opted to fly low and take a different approach to Tani's place. They landed in her back yard, out of sight of the street, and made their way to the back door.

A sharp knock on the door brought their first target

bustling over. "Whoever you are, you get out of my—" She stopped to gape. "What do you want! Are you robbing me? Fine. Take anything you want. Take it all." She backed away from the door, her hands raised and wings outstretched in panic.

"We're not robbing you. We just wanted to talk to you about Jenna. Your neighbor."

The female's voice was little more than a squeak. "Is she okay? What happened? I saw healers going inside."

Zanyr cleared his throat in surprise. Tani seemed legitimately concerned, which was unexpected. "She will be. Uh, thanks for asking. I'm curious why you're worried, though. I saw the way you looked at her yesterday. You don't like her much."

"Oh, that." The female looked down at her feet. "I probably owe her an apology. She's so... so... popular! Since she's moved in, no one gives me the time of day anymore. It's all Jenna this and Jenna that. She's got Sanjin's interest. That's for sure. He and I haven't been anything for a while now, but then she moves in, and he's all sorts of interested. Yesterday you two arrive with her, and, well." She huffed. "I was envious. Which is pathetic, I know. I mean, she doesn't even have wings! What do I have to be jealous of?"

"So yesterday's behavior was because you think she's getting too much attention?" Torren asked.

"Yes. Especially from Sanjin. I thought he actually liked me. I mean, clearly we're not fated for each other, but that doesn't mean we can't enjoy each other's company. Then last winter he suddenly announces he's got an *anrik*, and he's not interested in spending time with me anymore. In fact, he doesn't talk to anyone these days. Hasn't in ages. It's like he's a different male."

"Sanjin is the one with the little produce stand out in front of his house?"

Tani nodded. "That's the one. He used to live a block over, but he moved this spring. Dug up his garden and all his trees and replanted them in the new place. Told anyone who asked that the soil drained better at the new place. I have no idea what that means." She heaved a sigh. "I thought maybe he wanted to start things up again, but he barely speaks to me anymore."

Tani gave them a once-over that left Zanyr feeling thankful he was wearing thick, heavy armor. "I don't suppose the two of you are... available?"

"We're not," Zanyr said so fast he almost tripped over his tongue.

"We're mated. To Jenna. In fact, we should check on her. Make sure she's feeling better," Torren made for the door with Zanyr right behind him. It was time for a tactical retreat.

The female followed them to the porch, but once they were out in the yard, she raised a hand and closed the door.

"That was..."

"Never to be mentioned again," Torren said.

"Right." Zanyr was in full agreement.

"I think we need to have a chat with Sanjin next."

"I agree. Even if we disregard the gossip and excessive sharing of information, something's off there." Zanyr thought back to the produce he'd seen. He got the feeling he wasn't seeing the full picture, but what he could see, he didn't like.

"Hey, isn't he the one who gave Jenna the fruit she was raving about?"

"Son of a starbeast. You don't think..."

Neither of them finished that sentence. They both took to the air. It was time to get some answers.

This time, they didn't bother with subtlety. Then flew straight over the road and down into the neighbor's front yard. The second they touched down, they ran for the door and started to pound on it.

No one answered. "I'll head around back," Zanyr offered. No way he wanted this male to slip away now. Even as he ran, he spotted Skye and several other palace guards headed their way.

The back door was locked. Lights were on inside, but he didn't see any movement.

"Sanjin Tav, in the name of the prince and the leadership council, come out. Now!" Skye shouted.

Still no movement. A bad feeling crawled down his spine and settled into his stomach. Was he already gone? Or was an innocent male cowering under his bed, wondering what the *fraxx* was going on?

"We're going in. If he bolts, he's coming straight at you. Be ready," Torren sent.

The crash of a battering ram tore through the air. Someone shouted. Footsteps sounded from inside the house. Then. Nothing.

Zanyr waited. And waited some more. This wasn't right. The bad feeling intensified.

"*Fraxx*! Get a medic in here now!" Skye barked the order from somewhere inside.

Finally, the back door opened. Torren stood there, looking frustrated and furious.

"Well?" Zanyr asked.

Torren gestured for him to follow. "Come inside. You need to see this."

One look in the dead male's bedroom made it obvious why he didn't want visitors, especially ones looking to spend time in bed with him. There was no bed. Instead, there was a cryo-pod, a desk, an array of monitors, and recording equipment.

"We found our spy." Skye stood by the cryo-pod. Lights flashed across the main panel, and the viewport was obscured by heavy frost.

"He's in there?" Zanyr asked.

"He is," Skye confirmed. "It looks like he put himself into cold storage after the attack on Jenna."

"Wake him up. I want to have a word with the *bakaffa*." Zanyr curled his hands into fists and stomped toward the pod.

Skye intercepted him, using her body to block his path. "Whoa. You're in no state to interrogate anyone."

He briefly contemplated pushing past her, but he'd gone up against enough cyborgs in the practice arena to know the odds were not in his favor. He was a warrior. Skye was a living weapon. He stopped in front of her and growled.

The cyborg's mouth quirked up at one corner. "I know you're pissed, Zan. But growling at me won't help the situation."

She was right. He blew out a breath and bowed his head to her. "Sorry."

"I get it. If someone went after Yardan, I'd want to tear open that pod and get some answers."

Torren joined them. "How long until we can get him out of there?"

"That depends on what I see on the scanner." A massive male entered the room, forcing several of the guards to flatten themselves against the walls to make room. Zanyr didn't need to see his face to know who it was. Only one being in the colony was that size. Denz, the half-Torski who sat on the leadership council with him. Why were they all showing up today? Had he missed a memo or something?

"Denz," he greeted the male.

He got a nod in return, but nothing more. Instead, Denz raised his voice. "Everyone not on the leadership council needs to clear the area. Now. And no talking to anyone about this until you've been debriefed."

"Come on, let's go find Yardan. He'll want to talk to all of you." Skye led the others out of the room.

Torren made to follow, but Denz stopped him. "Not you. You might as well hear it now instead of Zan telling you later."

"I don't tell him everything," Zanyr protested.

Despite the circumstances, Denz looked at him with amusement. "This involves your *mahaya*. If you withheld information from Torren, we'd be investigating another violent crime."

"True," Torren said.

They waited until the house was clear before anyone

spoke again. In the meantime, Denz used a medical scanner to gather data from the pod and its occupant. His expression, already serious, grew increasingly grim as he read the results.

"*Fraxx.* I didn't want to be right about this," Denz said.

"What is going on?" Zanyr asked.

Denz sighed. "Zan, you already know some of this. Do you remember when the Shadow Men infiltrated the orbital platform?"

Zanyr nodded. "One of our shuttle pilots was offering information in exchange for a narcotic capable of affecting someone with Vardarian nanotech. His contact was hiding in plain sight on the platform."

"The suspect was actually a digitized consciousness in a cloned body," Denz said.

Torren jerked and stared at the cryo-pod. "Are you saying this is another clone being driven around by a digital ghost? So what? Right now we have the body, but whoever is operating it is not home right now?"

"That's one way to put it." Denz tried to smile, but it faded quickly. "At least this time there's no micro-explosives. Sanjin, or whoever is controlling this body, has no means to destroy the evidence."

Zanyr stood in silence as his mind worked to put the pieces together. Sanjin's sudden change in personality. The way he'd retreated from Tani. Even the fact he'd moved to be closer to what would be Jenna's new home. "We need to find out how he knew where Jenna would be living."

"We will. It will take time, but we'll figure out every place he went and everyone he spoke to."

Something else clicked for Zanyr. "The produce he's selling. Get someone to test it all. I bet you'll find he's been using banned products and techniques to grow everything."

Torren shot him a quizzical look. "Are you still thinking about fruits right now?"

"I am. Because I think it might help us confirm when Sanjin stopped being Sanjin. The original was a gardener. I bet whoever was driving him didn't know anything about agriculture, so they used shortcuts and cheats to make it look like he knew what he was doing."

"His *anrik!*" Torren said. "Supposedly he works on the platform. We need to get him before he gets away."

"The platform and all vessels are already locked down. We'll find him."

Zanyr slammed his fist against his thigh in fury. "And then we need to look for others. What if they weren't the only ones here?"

Denz's expression turned stormy. "Then we find them, remove them, and send a message to these bastard Shadow Men to leave us, and our colony, alone."

That was a message Zanyr could get behind.

17

"Will you stop fussing!" Jenna protested as Torren tried to fluff her pillow again.

"The healers said you needed to rest for at least another day." Torren finished what he was doing and then sat down next to her on a couch bigger than most of the rooms she'd lived in during her time on Earth.

"That's what they told *you*. Jodi said I was the best judge of when I was ready to be up and around. This is me, telling you, I am more than ready."

Two days at the med-clinic and another day sitting around her new home was enough to drive her to distraction. She'd never spent this much time sitting around, doing nothing. Even on the voyage here she'd kept busy studying languages, taking classes with the other women, and exercising to help her muscles prepare for Liberty's higher gravity.

"Why would they give us different instructions?" Zanyr stood by the window, his body highlighted by the rays of the setting sun.

"I thought that would be obvious. We were only in the second day of the *sharhal* when I got sick. Sure, the transfusion you did eased my symptoms, but there wasn't much they could do for the two of you. They were concerned your needs might make you rush me."

Torren growled. "They lied to us to make sure we didn't bed you too soon? Do they think so little of our control? I'm going to tie that *bakaffa* healer to a post and show him what it looks like when I lose control!"

"No, you won't, because I was always the one who had the final say, and I say I'm done waiting."

Both males straightened, their scales tightening in response. "You're sure?" Zanyr asked.

"Yes! Very. Totally. Utterly. Completely certain." She threw off the blanket she'd been nestled under since lunch. Zanyr had only come in from the fields a little while ago, which was why she'd waited this long. Now that they were both here, she was done waiting.

"You heard our *ana-thi*. She doesn't want to wait any more." Torren swept her into his arms so quickly she barely felt her feet leave the ground.

"Thank the ancestors." Zanyr had one foot up and was pulling off one of his socks while also attempting to undo his pants one-handed. It seemed they were done waiting, too.

Torren muscled past him and carried her up the stairs. They hadn't flown with her since the incident, but they had insisted on carrying her everywhere. Flying was something else she wanted to do again. Soon.

She really was recovered. In fact, she'd never felt this good in her life. It had taken the nanotech a full day to repair the damage done to her heart, but after that, her recovery had been amazingly swift.

At first, the healers thought she'd been poisoned. The truth only came out when her bloodwork revealed minute traces of a type of medi-bot no one had seen before. It was very similar to the ones the corporations used on their cyborgs, but it had been modified in several ways.

For one thing, it was so close a match to the standard technology that normal medi-bots wouldn't have recognized it as a threat. Even if she had taken the medi-bot treatment already, it wouldn't have saved her.

For another, it appeared the tech had a single purpose. Once activated, the miniature swarm attacked her cardiac muscles, starving them of blood flow and oxygen until the cells died. If Torren and Zanyr hadn't found her, she'd have died from what would have looked like a sudden heart attack. While uncommon for someone her age, it wasn't unheard of. Sanjin could have killed her, and no one would have realized it. Everyone assumed that was his plan. If things had gone the way he intended, he would have returned to the body and continued as usual.

The investigation was still ongoing, but they now knew at least two of the cloned abominations were in the colony. Sanjin was one, and Kabar, the one he referred to as his *anrik*, was the other. Kabar worked on the orbital platform, but records indicated he hadn't been down to the planet for several months. He met with Sanjin on his last trip to the planet. They had undergone the bonding ceremony, and then they'd never seen each other again.

Kabar's cabin had been destroyed with an acid bomb, denying investigators the chance to go through his things. He'd wiped his files, too, scrubbing them so well that not even Phaedra and her cyber-team had been able to recover anything. The body, or what was left of it, was sprawled on the floor in a tangle of limbs.

The digitized consciousnesses in control of the two clones had escaped, leaving Haven's citizens with more questions than answers. What little they did know did not bode well for the colony. They had been infiltrated by the enemy. Haven was under attack in the same way Sanjin had tried to kill her—from the inside.

Torren's kiss pulled her out of her thoughts and back to the present. "Come back to me, blossom."

"I'm here." She cupped his face in her hands and kissed him back. It was the same thing she'd been trying to say while she'd lain on the floor, fighting for her next breath. She'd heard them calling her, asking her to come back, to stay with them. She'd tried so hard to answer, but she hadn't been able to say it then.

"Good." Zanyr joined them. "I'd hate for you to miss this next bit."

She laughed and reached out to swat his shoulder. "I don't think this would work without me here."

Torren set her down by the bed and drew her into his arms while Zanyr moved in behind her. Once again she found herself sandwiched between her two males, only this time she knew exactly what would happen next.

They stripped her quickly, which turned out to be one of the advantages to the Vardarian style of clothing.

"Easy access," they'd told her when she'd opened the box of new clothes they'd bought for her.

They didn't stop until all three of them were naked, their clothes piled up on the floor at their feet. She was caught between them, lost to a storm of sensation as they caressed and tasted every part of her they could reach.

One of them brushed a hand over the *harani* she now wore. They had waited for her to be ready before completing their claiming, but they hadn't been idle. First, they had presented her with a dagger. It was Torren's favorite, and the one he'd used to break the glass so they could reach her.

This morning, they'd exchanged armbands. A set of three, identical except in size. Three strands of gold were braided together, each of them with a stylized emblem of a falling star. The bands marked them as a mated trio, and the falling star was a way of reclaiming their past and forging it into something new.

"I like the way this looks on our female," Torren said.

"And the female likes it very much as well. But she likes the way the two of you wear yours even better. Now everyone will know you are claimed. Especially Tani."

Zanyr claimed her mouth with a kiss that left her breathless. "We should never have told you about that. I thought we agreed to never mention it again, Vex."

"You also promised to always tell me the truth," she reminded him.

"And we always will," Torren said, his mouth near her ear. "Now, truthfully, blossom. What do you need from us?"

She shivered as his voice slid across her skin and into her soul.

"I need you to claim me. To make me yours in every way. I want to give myself to you both."

"Oh, yes, *mahaya*. We will do that. And what will you give us?" Torren asked.

"Everything," she whispered. "Including my submission."

Both males growled, the sound rolling through her like thunder. They led her to the bed, helping her up onto the mattress and positioning her so she was kneeling on the bed. Torren moved behind her, his hands on her hips and the heavy length of his cock pressed against the swell of her ass.

He kissed his way up her spine as Zanyr slid into place beneath her, coaxing her legs apart until she was straddling his hips.

Zanyr reached up and back, and she heard a drawer open and then close again.

"What's that?" she asked as she spotted him holding a small vial.

"*Uli* oil. It will make everything more intense."

He poured a little onto one palm and then handed the vial to Torren. Zanyr rubbed it between his hands and then cupped her breasts, letting the oil slide over her skin.

She moaned at the exquisite sensation and then moaned again when Torren poured more of it over her back and buttocks. He stroked his fingers through the oil, drawing patterns of pleasure all over her body. When he reached between her legs she rocked backward, eager for his touch.

He teased her clit for a moment and then retreated, letting his fingers glide along the seam of her ass cheeks. "All you have to do is let us love you, blossom. Trust us with your pleasure."

"I will," the answer came easily, without doubt or reservation.

Both males groaned.

Zanyr took over pleasuring her clitoris while Torren slowly worked the oil into new places. It was unfamiliar but not unpleasant, and soon Jenna found herself rocking between their touch. In and out, back and forth. She found the rhythm of their dance and followed where they led her.

Zanyr claimed her first, replacing his fingers with the thick crown of his cock. She lowered herself over him, feeling him part her body as he slid into her depths with a shuddering growl.

She kissed him, drinking in the sound and reveling in the power she had over him at this moment.

When Torren pressed a finger inside her, she felt nothing but pleasure. When he added another, she followed his instructions and simply allowed herself to flow between them, finding new levels of ecstasy at every turn.

By the time Torren slid into her dark entrance, she was drunk with pleasure. All she could do was cling to Zanyr, her fingers gripping the sheets and her mouth mated to Zanyr's as the three of them moved together.

She was on the brink of release when they bit her,

coordinating the movement through a link she'd be able to share with them soon.

Torren bit her on the shoulder while Zanyr sank his fangs into a spot on the side of her neck. The initial flash of pain transformed into such perfect pleasure that she came with a cry.

Tears fell from her eyes as she felt them reach their peaks in the next few seconds, their fangs still sunk into her flesh and their blood mingling with hers.

She already carried their nanotech, and she wore her *harani* with pride, but now she had something else of theirs. The bites would scar into mating marks. And she'd wear them for the rest of her life. Forever marked. Forever claimed. Forever theirs.

"I love you," she told them as they slowly eased themselves free of her body before collapsing on either side of her.

"And we love you," they said the words together.

Torren kissed away her tears. "No matter what threats may come our way, we will always be with you. You are our gift, and we will protect you, always."

Zanyr touched the symbol on her armband, his smile tender and his eyes alight with love. "Until the last star falls."

***

Thank you for reading Her Alien Mercenaries.

I hope you enjoyed Jenna, Torren, and Zanyr's story.

Would you like to read a special bonus epilogue to this story? Sign up for my newsletter here: subscribepage.io/Bonuscontent

If you're looking for more stories like this one, I invite you to explore the other books in the <u>Drift</u> universe, which now Include Haven Colony, <u>Nova Force</u> and the original <u>Drift</u> series.

ABOUT THE AUTHOR

Susan lives out on the Canadian west coast surrounded by open water, dear family, and good friends. She's jumped out of perfectly good airplanes on purpose and accidentally swum with sharks on the Great Barrier Reef.

If the world ends, she plans to survive as the spunky, comedic sidekick to the heroes of the new world, because she's too damned short and out of shape to make it on her own for long.

To contact her about her books or to arrange end of the world team-ups, you can email her at susan@susanhayes.ca.

For all titles by Susan Hayes, please visit her website:
susanhayes.ca

To keep up with her latest news, releases, and appearances you can join her
Newsletter

Stay in Touch
Sign up for Susan's Newsletter